What did the cryptic message from Hong Kong mean?

To Mr. Lowry, it meant that his son, Dino, who disappeared three years before, might still be alive—somewhere . . .

To Marcia Lowry, Dino's wife, it meant that her plans to remarry were suddenly thrown into chaos . . .

To Richard Blake, Marcia's fiancé, it meant that he might suddenly lose the girl he loved . . .

To them all, it would mean much more: baffling suspense, terror and murder!

MIGNON G. EBERHART

MESSAGE FROM HONG KONG

POPULAR LIBRARY • NEW YORK

Published by Popular Library, CBS Publications,
CBS Consumer Publishing, a Division of CBS Inc., by
arrangement with Random House, Inc.

August, 1977

Copyright © 1968, 1969 by Mignon G. Eberhart

Library of Congress Catalog Card Number: 69-16421

ISBN: 0-445-04032-7

ONE

❀ ❀ ❀

The message came from Hong Kong late on an August afternoon. We had been swimming and were sitting on the grass beside the pool. We were not talking of Dino, yet Dino was on the fringe of all our talk; he had to be there.

"Our own home before Christmas," Richard said. "When are you going to tell your father-in-law?"

"He's had a bad two weeks. Let him get stronger."

He took me by the arm and swung me around to face him. I said, faltering, "It's so hard to tell him."

"Everything is arranged. You can't put it off any longer."

"I'm the only one he has."

There was a spark of anger in his eyes. "Do you really want to marry me?"

I leaned my head against his wet brown shoulder. "Oh, Dick, you fool, you."

His shoulder was unyielding. "Is Dino still on your mind?"

"I don't want Dino back. I'd like to be sure that he's—all right."

"He's been gone nearly three years. If he's still alive, he'd have come back by now. Because," Richard said ruthlessly, "he'd have run out of money. I think he's dead."

"Mr. Lowry thinks he will come back—"

"All right, do you intend to sacrifice what you want and what I want to save Mr. Lowry's feelings?"

"No. No—"

He was inexorable. "You were to tell him a month ago. You were to tell him last night."

"He'd gone to bed," I said weakly.

He released my arm and began to get up. "We'll tell him now."

"Oh, Dick, wait . . . he did have a bad attack—"

"Two weeks ago, and it wasn't all that bad. Come on—"

"But, Dick, it's a week before I'm supposed to leave and—"

"Do you really want to make a martyr of yourself?" he said very soberly.

"No! It's only that he has been like a father to me. A real father, the only one I ever knew, really."

"He's Dino's father, in fact. He's only your father-in-law. Let's have it out once and for all. Take your choice. Mr. Lowry or me. I want you, Marcia. I'm not going to have you dashing off away from me and our home every time Mr. Lowry gets the vapors."

"It's his heart—"

"Make up your mind," he said and meant it.

I said, "All right. I'll tell him now. He suspects, anyway."

"He knows. I can see it in his eyes. He can't stand the sight of me," Richard said bluntly and, as a matter of fact, truly. Mr. Lowry had been friendly enough when Richard came back to see us the previous Christmas. Lately he'd been watching me like a cat. Lately he'd taken to feeling ill when he knew that I intended to go out with Richard.

"You can't blame him," I said, winding up my wet hair, and then we both heard Mrs. Clurg panting down the path from the house.

So the message from Hong Kong came one week before I was to go to another state, take up residence there and later, in November, marry Richard. We both turned as if we had a premonition, but we hadn't; I thought that Mr. Lowry had had another attack. Mrs. Clurg rounded the enormous old lilac and cried, "He's heard from Dino! It came just now! Special delivery and air mail from Hong Kong . . ."

There was a very still moment. Mrs. Clurg wiped her hot face. Then Richard said, "All right, now we'll get things straight. Come on, Marcia."

I don't think I could have walked up the graveled path to the house without Richard's hand under my arm. There was no breeze on the path and no breeze on the wide, old-fashioned porch, but all at once, when I saw Mr. Lowry, my wet bathing suit became very clammy and cold. He had brown wrapping papers strewn about his wheelchair. His blue eyes were glistening with pleasure and perhaps with triumph. Dino was my husband, Daniel Lowry, and he had been gone, no one knew where, for nearly three years. We had last heard from him in Bangkok, a postal card. Since then there had been nothing at all. Mr. Lowry had made inquiries, everywhere, it seemed to me; nobody knew anything of him.

My knees were shaking. I sat down in one of the Chinese peel chairs which somebody had sent to Mr. Lowry from Hong Kong years ago.

"It's from Dino. I always knew he was alive. It's from Dino. Look—" He held a piece of pale-green, almost white jade in his hands. Mr. Lowry's hands always trembled a little; they were now pathetically unsteady.

Richard asked, "Where is Dino?"

Mr. Lowry shot an icy glance at him. "I don't know exactly. But I do know that Mr. Chen knows something of him."

"Mr. Chen?"

"This piece of jade came from him. Here's his name on the wrapping paper."

"Is that all there was? Nothing written? Just that—that thing?"

"That thing, as you call it, is a piece of jade."

"I know," Richard said patiently. "But why do you think it has anything to do with Dino?"

My father-in-law shot another stabbing, frigid look at Richard. "I know Mr. Chen. He's old. He must be ancient. But he had some reason for sending me this, and the reason is Dino. I'm going out to Hong Kong to find Dino."

Richard sat down slowly on the railing, his long legs doubled up. He mopped at a trickle of water down his neck. "Who is Mr. Chen?"

Mr. Lowry eyed Richard coldly and yet again with a touch of triumph. Mr. Lowry was observant; he liked me and I loved him, but Dino was his son. He said, "Mr. Chen was the Hong Kong agent for me and for my father when he had an importing business. The business was ended when I retired. Mr. Chen is of the old China. He is not of the new China. You'll remember, Dino went out to Hong Kong a couple of times to wind up the ends. So Mr. Chen knows him. Mr. Chen has a long memory. He values friendship above all things. He is an honorable man. Mr. Chen knows something about Dino."

Richard wiped his wet brown hand on his wet brown thigh. "But, Mr. Lowry," he said carefully, "if this Mr. Chen knows something about Dino, wouldn't he tell you so, directly?"

Mr. Lowry's rather purple lips curved downward. "You don't know the Chinese. I'm not sure that I do, as a matter of fact. It's been a long time since I was out there myself. But this means something. The wrapping had Mr. Chen's name on it."

"But not his address?" Richard said, very carefully.

"That doesn't matter. Tell me any other reason why he would send me this." Mr. Lowry held up the small rectangle of jade, and adjusted his spectacles in order to scrutinize it. "Of course, I know nothing about jade," he began and I knew that he was going to show off a little. He had a curious fund of knowledge which darted here and there, pouncing upon some subject that interested him. Now it was going to be jade. "It's not *feits' yu*."

"Huh?" Richard said, startled.

It would not be kind or respectful to shake my father-in-law and tell him to get to the point. He sensed my impatience, for he said rather hurriedly, "So-called Imperial jade. Not always of the Imperial treasure but gem jade, or, as some call it, king-fisher jade. This is pale green nephrite."

"Mr. Lowry!" Richard said like an explosion.

"Look for yourself." Mr. Lowry held the small medallion toward us. It was indeed the palest shimmering green; two animals that looked like deer were beautifully carved on it, with foliage in the background.

"It's an old piece," Mr. Lowry said. He touched it delicately. "You love jade only when you learn its touch. The point is that Mr. Chen sent it to me, out of the blue, and there's meaning to it and that is Dino. Whatever Mr. Chen knows I've got to know."

There was a little pause. We could hear Mrs. Clurg's footsteps on the gravel, climbing up slowly from the swimming pool. Richard said again in a quiet, almost gentle voice, "Why not write to Mr. Chen? Why not phone him?"

Mr. Lowry looked angry, triumphant and exasperated. "My dear Dick, Chen is not an uncommon name. It's like Jones or White or—why, there must be dozens of Chens in Hong Kong. I told you there's simply no address on the wrapping. Only his name: Chen Ho Lung."

Richard thought that over and Mrs. Clurg's footsteps rattled nearer. She paused, probably to take a breath. Richard asked absently, "Why do you call him Mr. Chen?"

"Because that's his name," Mr. Lowry said testily. "The surname comes first. No, there's no use talking to me, I've got to go to Hong Kong and see Mr. Chen. I intend to find Dino."

I decided that I really must go into the house and get out

of my clammy, chilly bathing suit and said, "No, it's all right, Father. I'll go to Hong Kong."

Richard stood up and said, "No!"

Mr. Lowry looked up with a flash of blue eyes, so like but so unlike Dino's eyes. He then icily put the thing in a nutshell. "If Dino is alive, and I believe that he is, I should not need to remind you, Dick, that Marcia is his wife."

Richard stood like a rock and looked at Mr. Lowry. It was almost as if Richard and I had been waiting for exactly that, a jade message from Hong Kong. He said, "We have been wanting to tell you, Mr. Lowry. Dino has been gone for nearly three years. Marcia has heard nothing from him. That is desertion. Marcia is going to marry me. She is to leave next week. Everything has been arranged—"

Mr. Lowry shot up from his chair and then collapsed, just a little too feebly and touchingly, but he said in a strong voice, "I've got eyes in my head. You needn't talk about any divorce. Oh, I understand it all right; I've seen this coming. In our state the so-called Enoch Arden law still obtains, seven years to wait before death is legally assumed to have occurred. Marcia can go to another state. She might get a divorce on the grounds of desertion. My opinion is that she does not want to get a divorce that way."

"I—" I began.

Mr. Lowry went straight on, "She thinks it right and fair to give Dino another chance."

Richard said suddenly, "No, she doesn't. He's had—"

Mr. Lowry took it away from him, too. "Marcia can get a divorce, certainly, any time. You two can marry. But Dino is alive, I'm sure of it now, and when he comes back, your marriage would be no marriage at all."

"Legally—" Richard began, but Mr. Lowry waved one hand. "You could find some legal standing, certainly," he said. "But how about your own feelings if, say, Dino returns in a few weeks, a year, any time, knowing nothing of your divorce and marriage? Legally perhaps, but morally—oh, there's no use saying things you know and Marcia knows. We've always believed Dino was kidnapped."

"Wait a minute, Mr. Lowry, you believed that, Marcia didn't—"

"It's the only answer. The only reason Dino would stay away so long."

"You had no demand for ransom—"

"That doesn't mean anything! There are a hundred reasons

why we never received a ransom demand. A thousand reasons! No, you'll see I'm right. Dino was kidnapped somewhere in Thailand or—or Cambodia or—"

"You don't know where he went," Richard said.

I made a little silencing gesture with my hand. I couldn't help it. Mr. Lowry's face was beginning to flush darkly red. Richard paid no attention to me. Mr. Lowry said, "None of that matters! I tell you Mr. Chen knows something about him and Dino needs help." He caught his breath in a loud gasp. Richard looked at me and I shook my head a little, meaning "Don't upset him so much," and Mr. Lowry said in a trembling voice, "Dino is my son. There were things that divided us, yes. All that is in the past. He's my son and I want him back. I'm going to Hong Kong."

Then Mrs. Clurg advanced. The floor of the old porch shook under her tread. She had been the housekeeper since Dino was a child; we now shared the housekeeping and the care of Mr. Lowry. Mrs. Clurg had an indisputable authority in the Lowry house. She said to me, "You'll catch your death, Marcia. Go put on dry clothes. As for going to Hong Kong, Mr. Lowry—" She gave a snort. "The very idea!"

In the end that summed it up; and the plain fact was that if Dino were alive, or if he needed help, then somebody had to find him and I was that person. One night before I left Mr. Lowry put it into words.

We were sitting on the porch again, having coffee, watching the moonlight which turned the cracked old swimming pool, built in the days of affluence, into a deceiving but pleasant sheet of silver. Mr. Lowry said abruptly, "Dick Blake doesn't want you to go out to Hong Kong. I'd rather go myself, yes. But somebody's got to do what can be done. Dino and I parted in anger. I regret that now. I'm an old man," said Mr. Lowry, in a pathetic way which was only a little overdone. I loved him but I knew him too. He went on quickly, as if he too knew that he was overdoing it a bit, "And as for you, my dear, you cannot think of marriage to Dick until you at least have some certain knowledge of Dino, until in fact you see him, for I know, I tell you, I know that he's alive."

I said nothing to that. During those few weeks Richard and I had talked endlessly on it; the jade could mean nothing, it could mean anything; there was nothing certain about

Mr. Lowry sipped his coffee. The pool and the shrubs and the lawn were silver; it was deep shadow where we sat.

Finally Mr. Lowry went on, "I can't beg you to give Dino another chance. But if you will—" I must have made some sharp gesture, for he said quickly, "No, no, don't say anything now. I won't ask you to promise. We both know Dino's—shortcomings. But suppose he's changed. Suppose he's what I've always wanted him to be. Suppose he's the Dino you married, my dear."

"He's older," I said, thinking, He never was the Dino I thought I married.

Mr. Lowry took it the wrong way. "Certainly he's older. He's come to his senses. I won't urge you. But only consider it. Consider how much marriage may mean to him now. Consider what it means to me. You're like a daughter to me. I know, I feel in my heart, that no matter how you think you feel about Dick Blake, just now—still, you are Dino's wife." He leaned over to put his shaky and pathetic hand on mine. "Marriage is marriage. I know you. I know that you'll give Dino another chance."

I picked up the coffee tray and went inside. Mr. Lowry was too intelligent not to know exactly when to stop and of course he thought he'd won, which he hadn't, but it would have been foolish of me to deny that he had not underlined my own obligation to him and not to Dino, but to marriage. I owed nothing to Dino and I did not think he had changed for the better.

I did hope to discover something of Dino which would answer the question of his disappearance and would satisfy Mr. Lowry. I did not want to discover that, in fact, Dino had been killed in some way which (unless Mr. Chen could inform us) we would never know. I had never wanted to know that Dino was dead. If he had deserted me of his own volition, that was, in a queer way, his business. If he had been kidnapped, as Mr. Lowry insisted, then obviously I had to do something to help him. But I didn't try to deceive myself. My strong and urgent motive for wanting to go to Hong Kong was to clear the way for my marriage to Richard as straightforwardly perhaps and as decently as I could.

Mr. Lowry, in spite of retirement and in spite of illness, always knew somebody who knew somebody; he gave me a letter to the Governor General of the Crown Colony of Hong Kong.

I already had a passport, for Aunt Loe had sent me the

money for a trip to England the previous summer to visit her. I had my smallpox certificate for re-entry. I had to take one or two more immunizations and in fact was feeling just slightly feverish and unhappy when Richard drove me to Kennedy Airport.

"It's a wild-goose chase," he said, looking out at the silvery plane. Passengers were straggling along near us. Richard suddenly put an arm around me as if to hold me back, whether or not.

"I have to go," I said.

"You mean you're going to go, come hell or high water." He then, rather to the astonishment of an elderly clergyman and the pleasure of a neat little woman in a feathery hat, took me into his arms. I could see the clergyman's wide eyes and the little woman's smile over Richard's shoulder. He turned my face to his. "I love you, Marcia. Now then—" Instead of further tender sentiments which I expected and indeed, wanted, he said practically, "Now you know what to do. First you're to go to the American consulate. Then you're to present the letter Mr. Lowry gave you to the Governor General. He'll probably pave the way for you to inquire of the police. Practically every big newspaper and magazine has a bureau there. Newsmen are very intelligent and alert. One of them may have picked up something."

"Mr. Lowry said to keep it away from the newspapers—"

"Mr. Lowry is a stubborn old—well, never mind. If you can't find Mr. Chen, you're to come straight home. No use in your trying to find Dino if you can't find Chen. Even if you do find him and he does know something of Dino, you're to come home. I'll see to the rest of it . . ." Then he kissed me and I went through the gate and onto the plane, and I had a calm and surprisingly quick trip to San Francisco, Honolulu and Tokyo, and finally landed at Kai Tak Airport in Hong Kong.

TWO

I settled into one of the world's luxury hotels in Kowloon (Richard had cabled for my reservation) and then went to the big officelike building on the Island which houses the American consulate. I talked to several helpful young men, was passed from one to another, and in the end one of them very kindly invited me to cocktails and advised me to go home. "Looking for a certain Mr. Chen is not like looking for a needle in a haystack," he told me over his gin and tonic. "It's more like looking for the right needle in a haystack jam-packed with needles. I'm sorry we have no record of your husband's having been here since his last visit—let me see, six years ago?"

"Yes. He came out twice that year to wind up his father's business." I had been seventeen then and dazzled by Dino.

"Yes. Well, at the time of your husband's disappearance, we had your father-in-law's letter of inquiry, but—"

"I know. The consulate had no information about him."

"There's been nothing since then, Mrs. Lowry. I'm sorry."

He invited me to dinner, which was kind too, and when I thanked him and said no, he told me I reminded him of his wife back home, and had red hair, too, only a more golden red. Mine, he said, was on the auburn side, but beautiful, he added hastily. It was all very pleasant and polite but did not lead to Mr. Chen or to Dino.

I sent Mr. Lowry's note to the Governor General and was invited to tea with him and his wife and they were kind, too, although in a different, rather parental way. The Governor General had a conversation over the telephone and made an appointment for me to see someone of the police; I never knew his title but he was obviously somebody of authority. When I arrived in his office he sent young British officers and young Chinese officers scurrying, looking through files, I assumed; the telephone books also had been consulted. Nobody had any record of a Daniel Lowry since his two business trips six years before; there was Mr. Lowry's letter of inquiry three years later and the police department's reply to the effect that there was no more-recent record concerning him. After he disappeared, we had sent out inquiries to the police and the American consulate in Hong Kong, as well as Bangkok, merely on the theory that he just might have gone on to Hong Kong.

The police officer said quietly that Hong Kong was a city of almost four million people. "Some of the Chens are in the telephone directory. Many of them don't have telephones."

Following up leads took more time than I had expected. Hong Kong is a busy city and that summer it was a rather uneasy city with its own problems. I had to make and then wait for appointments which eventually were courteously and kindly kept; indeed I met only courtesy and kindliness.

The hotel manager obligingly provided me with a young Chinese guide who had graduated from U.C.L.A. and spoke beautiful English and was very disappointed when I told him I had not seen a single baseball game that summer. There happened to be a tight pennant race in the American League and he was always immersed in a newspaper, but he also took me about Kowloon and Victoria Island and obviously felt that he should inform me of the Crown Colony. It was like a short course in history.

I did not expect to happen upon Dino. Yet I couldn't have helped looking for him in a subconscious kind of way, in the busy streets. I wasn't at all sure that if I did see him, I would recognize him, say, in black pajamalike clothing and a coolie hat. Not that the Dino I remembered would have worn such an outfit. I went alone to church on Sunday and watched the pomp and dignity with which the Governor General and his lady were ushered into the church, and thought how well the British do these things. England's sun has by no means set.

I became more familiar with Nathan Road in Kowloon, and I became bolder; I paid and thanked my young guide, took the Star Ferry myself to the Island and wandered around the main streets, among people of all nationalities probably, but mainly British and American tourists, American soldiers and sailors on leave, and Chinese. The day soon came when I saw that Richard was right; it was a fool's errand and I decided to go home. When I went down to the travel desk in the lobby, I was approached by a British merchant who was staying at the hotel.

There is, I suppose, a well-developed grapevine in any

popular tourist hotel. Probably by that time everyone in the hotel knew that I was trying to find a Mr. Chen, just as we all knew it when a tourist ran into or escaped some sporadic street fighting, or when there was a new rumor that the water, which everyone knew was piped in from China, was to be cut off. The British merchant had told me firmly on one occasion never to touch water but stick to gin, and that there was nothing to get in a flap about. An elderly Hollander did not agree with him, he had escaped with his life only from the Japanese invasion of Sumatra; he had recently been forced to leave Macao; he had lived in the East since he was eighteen; he knew no other home but he was tired and bitter. As I tucked the airline ticket in my handbag the British merchant, whose name I never knew, said to me, "I may have some news that will interest you, Mrs. Lowry. There's a little curio shop with the name Chen Ho Lung beside the door. I wondered if that could be the Mr. Chen you wish to see. It's a junk shop really, but it has a few nice things. I bought this for my wife." He pulled a little package from his pocket, unwrapped some wrinkled and soiled tissue paper and showed me a piece of smooth, pale jade. It was so pale that it was almost white. It was not, it could never have been an exact duplicate of the jade which had been sent to Mr. Lowry, but the design was again that of two animals against a background of foliage. The similarity was strong enough to suggest that once the two medallions might have been companion pieces.

The British merchant must have seen some change in my face, for he said, "Is anything wrong?"

"I think you may have found the right Mr. Chen. Where—"

He interrupted. "Well, now I think I'll just take you there. It's on the Island. Rather off the beaten path. Yes, I'll take you there."

We took the brief ferry ride from Kowloon to the Island of Hong Kong, and as always, the harbor was crowded with cargo ships, a destroyer or two, cruise ships, junks and houseboats. As always, the Island lifted to an abrupt peak; as always, the rising rows of new apartment buildings looked like the white icing between layers of a rather mixed-up cake.

We took one of the line taxis at the ferry, turned out of a main street and presently had to leave the taxi at the turn into a very narrow road. It was scarcely more than a footpath, yet it was crowded with people in ordinary Western clothes, in Chinese clothes, in the tag ends of any kind of garments which marked the refugees. It smelled. It was dusty. It was lined with fruit stalls and vegetable stalls which looked as if they had been put up for the day only and would be swept away at night. Yet I knew that some people slept huddled in shelters which by day kept the sun off their wares. My British friend wound his way comfortably through the men, women, children, dogs and stalls, and then stopped. He pointed to a panel beside an open door leading to a shop which looked like a hole in the wall. "Here we are." There were Chinese characters straggling down the panel; below, in small but to me comprehensible print, was the name Chen Ho Lung.

"I think it was an assistant who sold me the jade," my British friend said, as if warning me not to expect too much. "I think the proprietor was in the back of the shop." He added, with the typical British delicacy which permits one's own business to remain one's own business, "I'll wait outside."

So I went into the shop. The street had been narrow, crowded and dusty but sunny; the shop was narrow, crowded, dusty and dark. It was hung with a few guitars and banjos which seemed unlikely; there was a dusty glass case mainly full of sheer junk, sandalwood fans and bundles of incense sticks. In it were also some ashtrays and ornaments of what, from its lardy look, I thought was mutton-fat jade, and there were two buckles from old-time Mandarin robes of beautiful white jade, set with scissors and a paper knife to make a handsome desk set, but most of the contents of the case had a kind of hopeless and dusty look. The only shelf that was clean of dust, as if it saw some activity, was laden with a mysterious-looking medication called Tiger Balm. There was also what I can only describe as a Chinese smell, just a little musty, a little stale, and in the shop, permeated with sandalwood. Unexpectedly, somewhere in the air, there was also the faintest trace of a delicate and pleasant perfume which somehow seemed familiar. After a second I identified it; it was a trace of Chanel Number Five, so probably an American tourist, a woman, had visited the shop that morning. Oddly, I was rather pleased about that, for it indicated that the curio shop was not really so far off the beaten path, and I was not, really, so remote from fellow Americans.

As surprising as the guitars and banjos was a Coromandel screen which stood at the back of the shop, stately in its beauty; it seemed to be used for strictly ulititarian purposes, as it covered a space there. The presence of such a screen, far from its native India, perhaps a one-time maharaja's palace, and now in the back of a curio shop in Hong Kong, did not seem unusual; after even my short stay I had come to the conclusion that everybody and everything at some time touches or is touched by Hong Kong. Such is its cosmopolitanism and such too is the city's own particular seething and magnetic life. I called out, "Is anybody here?"

My heart was in my throat as I waited for Mr. Chen to emerge. There was a shuffle from behind the Coromandel screen. Then a thin, youngish-oldish man emerged, rolling down his sleeves of his flapping black blouse. He had reddish hair, bluish eyes and a yellowish mustache; he could not be Mr. Chen. There was something seedy about him, run-down and not caring, yet when he spoke, it was clearly with the accent of the British upper class. "Yes, madam?"

This, then, was the man my British friend had referred to as the assistant. "I was expecting—that is, I came to see Mr. Chen."

It seemed to me that there was a flicker in his faded blue eyes. He picked up a tattered piece of red silk and began to polish a glass case which certainly needed polish. "Oh, you saw the sign at the door. Mr. Chen died two years ago."

"But I heard from him—that is, my father-in-law heard from him only three weeks ago!"

He polished with the once lovely, now stained and ragged piece of red silk. "I'm sorry. You've made a mistake."

I had to insist; the airline ticket in my handbag made a last effort mandatory. "But we did receive a package, a piece of jade, from Mr. Chen only about three weeks ago. I am Mrs. Daniel Lowry. It was sent to Mr. Charles Lowry."

I was sure then that there was agitation in his swift glance and in his nervously polishing hands. He said, so quickly that he jumbled up the words, "No, no. Quite impossible. My name is George Hobson. Mr. Chen took me in when I was— needed work. Before he died he left the shop to me. Mr. Chen could not have sent anyone a piece of jade and I certainly know nothing of it—"

I interrupted. "But you did have a piece like it, a duplicate. You sold it only today. I saw it."

I half turned to call in the Englishman, who would verify my statement, at which Mr. Hobson said quickly, "Oh, yes. I remember. But that was the only piece of the kind I ever had. Really I can't be of any help to you . . ."

I had turned back to him. I fancied that my friendly escort had come to the door of the shop, because for just a fraction of a second the shop became darker, as if someone stood briefly in the doorway shutting out what little light there was. If so, the shadow passed.

Mr. Hobson put down the piece of red silk. His young-old face seemed more shrunken, his eyes nervous, and clearly he was determined to get rid of me. "Can I interest you in anything else, madam? No? Then . . ." He walked toward the door and I almost had to go to the door too. Before I knew it he was bowing me out. "Thank you, madam. I'm sorry. Good afternoon."

I was in the street when I heard the door close behind me, and then I heard, which was odd, the rasp of a bolt. Mr. Hobson did not seem to want customers.

The shrilling of voices, the murmur of feet, the rustle and bustle and dust of the street surrounded me again in a way which was a little confusing, and I could not see my friendly Englishman anywhere. A thin dog came up, looked at me without much hope and wandered off again. The door behind me remained closed and uncommunicative. Then I saw the Englishman sturdily but politely pushing his way between two wheelbarrows laden with cabbages. "Sorry. I went to look for someone. Was it the right Mr. Chen?"

"No. The man who sold you the jade said that Mr. Chen died two years ago." I was tired and discouraged and ready to go home.

He put a big hand at my elbow; we got through the dusty melee and back to a street where there was a taxi. Only when we were crossing to Kowloon and the hotel again the Englishman said, "I didn't mean to desert you. The fact is that someone came and looked into the shop door and—I don't know, there was something fishy about him."

THREE

There had been an impression of a shadow, lingering for only a second or two. I said, "Fishy?"

"I thought he was interested in your handbag," the Englishman said sensibly. "He moved away so fast—that I don't know, I followed him for a moment. But then he slid out of sight."

It was the word "fishy" that set off a tingle of curiosity; I could not help thinking of Dino. "What did he look like?"

I was surprised when my companion chuckled. "What you Americans call a beatnik type. Very fancy clothes, fuzzy beard, hair almost to his shoulders. Fattish—too old for such foolishness. Here we are."

Whoever it was, though, I had a notion that George Hobson had seen him in the doorway and therefore immediately bowed me out and shut the door after me. But whoever it was, it couldn't have been Dino—slim, handsome, debonair, having his clothes made by the most expensive tailor in New York because, said Dino, he liked real buttonholes in his coat sleeves, not fake ones. Yet Dino hadn't minded fakery about other things.

My British friend and I parted at the door to the bar after he had politely invited me to have a gin sling, which I was too disheartened to accept. "It'd do you good," he said and was probably right.

I went up to my room and packed for the next day's flight home. I hadn't much to pack but by the time I finished it was dark enough for me to see from my balcony the incredibly lovely lights of the Island, strung out against the darkness, red and blue and green along the quay, brilliant and white along the mountain drives where the new apartment houses stood. Somewhere in the black spaces between these were refugees' shacks. I had been far too intent on my own errand to listen to much talk of Hong Kong's political situation; nevertheless, I could not help sensing a kind of controlled tension, something simmering under the skin of the city. Yet, in

19

spite of occasional bombs or street riots, there was always a strong sense of an undisturbed modus vivendi; after all, a modern, busy, commercial city of nearly four million people must arrive at some way of living from day to day. As in any city, there were sure to be places, streets, which made and kept their own secrets; as in any city, the police must have known and watched and done their best to keep under control certain dark and ugly hiding places, but the tourist saw nothing of all that.

I watched the lights sparkle across the strip of water and thought of George Hobson. Certainly he had seemed nervous and uneasy, as if he didn't want to talk to me at all. This implied some knowledge of the jade piece which he was determined not to admit. Indeed, he had seemed so uneasy that it was almost as if he were afraid of something or someone. On the other hand, it was perfectly possible that he was telling the truth and that his uneasiness was caused by his seeing the beatnik type my British friend had described to me; thus Mr. Hobson had shut me out of his shop and locked the door against any felonious intent.

The sum of it was, however, that even if he knew something of the jade, he did not intend to talk about it. Any way I looked at it, it was a stalemate. I went downstairs, ate a dinner which was delicious, in spite of a new rumor that food supplies might be rationed, and went back up to my room. I did not see my British merchant friend again.

Morning was overcast, spitting a little rain, and I hoped it would clear before my afternoon flight. I picked up the telephone by my bed, intending to order breakfast, and then saw an envelope which had been pushed under my door. Probably the reason I thought instantly of George Hobson and the curio shop was that even from across the room the envelope looked wrinkled and dirty. I ran to pick it up and opened it. There was a short note beginning, "My dear Mrs. Lowry." It had been typed on an obviously old and battered machine. There was also a typed enclosure, at first glance a list of names. The note read:

My dear Mrs. Lowry:

Take this to your father-in-law. Mr. Chen would have wished it. That's why I sent the jade. Mr. Chen was a man of honor. He was good to me. I couldn't talk to you. Someone was listening. You shouldn't have come.

Go home. Nothing you can do. Very dangerous. Stay out of it. This is all I can do.

The note was not signed; no signature was necessary. Then I looked at the enclosure.

It was merely a short list of names and cities, all of them American; there were no addresses. I read the list over and over. The first entry was *John Smith*, then a jumble of letters and numerals, then *San Francisco*. There followed simply: *Herbert Jones, Tampa; Joseph Brown, Chicago; James Black, New York;* each name followed by a mixture of letters and numerals which seemed a random choice.

The names meant nothing to me, yet there had to be some connection between the names and Dino, for George Hobson was saying that Mr. Chen would have wished my father-in-law to have that list.

And Mr. Hobson said: "Go home. . . . Very dangerous. Stay out of it." I couldn't even guess what "it" was. So I ordered breakfast; I dressed and put the list and Mr. Hobson's note carefully in the zippered part of my handbag along with my airplane tickets and passport.

I believed George Hobson. I believed that he believed every word he had written. I believed that someone had been listening when I visited the shop the previous day, standing either behind the Coromandel screen or in the doorway until my British friend frightened him away. I believed all this. But one does not ordinarily quite believe in danger. It is a word that seems to be an exaggeration, nothing valid. To anyone living the kind of life most of us live, danger as a direct and physical fact is simply not comprehensible. So I went to see George Hobson.

I remembered the street, although it looked different, dreary and ugly, that drizzly morning. I dismissed the taxi. A fat tourist with a pink face and a camera plodded along near me and I was oddly grateful for his presence. I found the little curio shop.

I also found Mr. Hobson, but his young-old face was now dreadfully old and terrible, for Mr. Hobson lay behind the counter, his head on the dirty piece of red silk. Mr. Hobson would never explain his note to me or the list of names.

The tourist had followed me into the shop and I heard his gasp. "My God!" he said. "Good gracious! The man's dead. His throat's cut. All that blood! We must call the police.

Here, young lady!" He took me by the arm, looked wildly around, and I suppose saw no chair, for he simply lowered me to the floor and propped me against a showcase. Then he darted away. I shut my eyes and tried not to be sick. The tourist returned with a young Chinese policeman who must have been on point duty; I remember the long stretch of white reaching almost to his elbows. He ran behind the counter. The tourist explained what he could explain; he had seen me enter the shop; he had been immediately behind me. I didn't realize just then what a debt of gratitude I owed the tourist.

I wished I had never seen George Hobson; I wished I were safe at home. I wished the stuffy little room would not smell of sandalwood; I wished it would stop tilting around me. I fixed my gaze on the Coromandel screen, the only witness, standing in silence and beauty at the end of the shop, but unable to tell who murdered little George Hobson or why.

The policeman and the tourist were talking of looting, theft, someone who had killed George Hobson and got away. They were looking also for a knife which they did not find. The policeman looked also for a telephone, said something to the tourist and went quickly out of the shop. The tourist squatted down beside me and said it was dreadful, he'd never seen anything like this in Dayton, Ohio, and was I feeling any better? In a few moments two more policemen arrived, and the three of them were very efficient in their immediate tasks and stepped over me with apology and seemed to know exactly what to do. Within moments another man arrived, an Englishman, in a beige silk suit and sun helmet, in spite of the drizzle outdoors. He talked to the young Chinese policemen, he spoke to the tourist, he went behind the counter. I still sat hunched up on the floor and felt as if I had murdered withered little old-young George Hobson myself. It seemed to me that they must blame me, for I was to blame.

They didn't. They seemed only sorry and apologetic because I had come upon so dreadful a sight. The tourist from Dayton talked and listened. I just sat there, thinking of George Hobson, educated, a gentleman in his instincts, determined to pay his debt to Mr. Chen because Mr. Chen had taken him in when he needed help and given him all that he had to give; George Hobson had died, I was sure, because he had tried to help me and warn me of some danger which he had obviously been afraid to explain.

The policeman in the beige suit took me back to my hotel.

I knew only that they found no knife and that they had covered George Hobson and were waiting to take him away. The tourist remained, pink again and curious. The policeman proved to be an inspector. Somehow I got the impression, I don't know why, that he, rather than a Chinese officer, had been sent to start inquiries because the man from Dayton and I, two American tourists, friends of the British, were in a sense involved; if so, it was an unnecessary touch of police diplomacy, although I did find him easy to talk to, almost too easy. On the ferry I had to rouse myself and resolve to tell the inspector the truth but not all the truth.

The reason for my decision was rather dismally cogent. If George Hobson had been murdered because I was making inquiries about Dino, then Dino was certainly alive but in some kind of dangerous position himself. There were, unfortunately, two ways of looking at that danger. It was possible that Dino's kidnappers—if kidnappers there actually were—had gone as far as murder to prevent George Hobson from giving any information at all. But it was also possible that Dino had got himself involved in something which did not bear investigation; consequently Dino might need protection, from the police, perhaps from anyone.

And George Hobson had warned me of the danger; he had felt so strongly about it that he had found out where I was staying, which would be easy; he had slid that dirty envelope under the door of my room, which would not be so easy. How George Hobson, seedy and shabby had accomplished this could have a hundred explanations: for example, he could have sent a messenger, or he could have paid a hotel porter or bellboy to deliver the note. I only knew that he had done what he believed to be his duty; he had then been murdered.

Once we arrived at the hotel, the inspector took me to a quiet little bar which I had never chanced upon before, and without asking me ordered a brandy and soda. When it came he told me pleasantly to sip it slowly; I did and could almost feel the color come back to my face. I also happened to catch a glimpse of myself in a wall mirror, dark red hair pushed back, as if without knowing it I had shoved it up high over my temples, face white, eyes looking black and strange instead of plain gray, pinkish lipstick standing out. My gray travel suit, which looked like tweed but was really a travel silk, looked untouched, trim, straight from Fifth Avenue, as in fact it had been, but five years ago, a part of the trousseau

Aunt Loe had supplied, but it now seemed odd, out of place. It was not a suit in which to come upon a murder in a tiny curio shop in Hong Kong. But what kind of dress did one wear for murder? I checked that fancy, and in the same instant noticed my white washable gloves also looking very trim, untouched by anything like murder, but smeared on the palms by dust from the shop floor. I removed them. I saw the inspector glance at my hand with its wedding ring, and sipped my brandy and soda.

"That's better," the inspector said. He had pale, observant eyes, a long bony face and pale hair, plastered so neatly down that it shone. "Now then, Mrs. Lowry, is it? I thought you said 'Miss.' "

I shook my head and then nodded and sipped more brandy.

"You've had a shock. I do have to ask a few questions, but that's all. I really don't think you went to that shop and took a knife so very skillfully to the proprietor's throat."

FOUR

❀❀❀

"No, I didn't," I said flatly.

"It is an out-of-the-way place, isn't it? Mind telling me how you happened to come upon it? And why you went there this morning?"

The whole truth, I said to myself, up to a point. And as a matter of fact, much of my truth-telling was of no virtue, for I had already visited the police; there was certainly some record of my visit and my inquiries about Mr. Chen and about Dino. I sipped again and began, "I came out to Hong Kong to find a Mr. Chen. I went to the police, of course, and the American consulate and—you see, my husband, Dino, I mean Daniel Lowry, may have been kidnapped nearly three years ago."

His pale eyes sharpened. "Not in Hong Kong. I'd remember."

"We don't know where. We're not even sure that he was kidnapped. We never had a ransom demand. He'd gone to Thailand. We heard from him from Bangkok. Then he disappeared."

He seemed to think it over. "Well, it's true that in some parts of our world out here—not especially in Thailand, but some places—kidnapping is in some circles almost a respectable profession. However, do you mind telling me why he came out East?"

Dino went to get a new start, I thought coldly. He promised his father: a new start, a new business, a new life. "He hoped to start an import-export business. That was his father's business, and his grandfather's, tea and silk mainly from China in the beginning. Eventually, with the new regime in China my father-in-law gave up his Chinese sources of supplies. Later he retired."

"I see. Your husband hoped to start another business in the East. In his blood, logical."

There was another long pause. Then the inspector asked with a shade of embarrassment, "Was there any possibility that your husband—well, disappeared of his own volition?"

"That is possible, yes." I heard my own voice, tired of that particular speculation.

The inspector ordered a pink lemonade. Then he said, delicately again, but hitting the next nail squarely on the head, "What about his money?"

"Dino had some money, not much, which his father gave him. Only to—to stake him for a while. It wouldn't have lasted three years."

"You heard nothing more at all?"

"Nothing, until the piece of jade came."

"Jade?"

So I went on, sticking to the exact truth; the jade piece, my reason for coming to Hong Kong, the futility of my inquiries, the piece of jade which my British friend had bought, our visit to the curio shop. Then I began to hedge a little, for I didn't tell him that George Hobson had all but pushed me out of the shop. I did not tell him about the note or the list which he had contrived to give me, or my notion that Dino must be alive, and that he might be involved himself in some sort of shady undertaking. If I had argued with myself about moral considerations, I could have told myself that I had, in fact, no real evidence of anything. I don't remember having any particular doubts of my own action. The inspector sipped his rather ghastly-looking drink and said, "I take it that Mr. Chen was one of the old-time Chinese."

"So my father-in-law said. We couldn't have cabled or written or telephoned to ask Mr. Chen what he meant by sending the jade. There was no address. Besides, my father-in-law said he understood it perfectly."

"Yes, well, I fancy your father-in-law was quite right. I've lived out here since I was a youngster. I knew some of the elderly Chinese and—yes, your father-in-law probably made the right interpretation. But George Hobson denied knowing anything about it. Curious." His pale eyes shifted to mine. "Why did you return to the curio shop this morning?"

Lies or half-lies can come with really shocking ease. "I have a reservation on the afternoon plane home. I went to the shop, thinking that if I talked to Mr. Hobson again, I might get some hint this time as to why the jade was sent in a wrapper with only Mr. Chen's name on it. It was my last chance." I swallowed hard. "He was lying there, you saw him . . ."

"Yes. Well—" He thumped his glass on the table and shot up. I heard it too; a loud crash and roar thundered through the hotel and rattled the glasses behind the bar. The barman ducked behind the counter. "Excuse me, Mrs. Lowry, for a moment," the inspector said as politely as if he were at a dinner party, and left.

The bartender stuck his head cautiously above the counter. I gulped. "What was that?"

"Another bomb." The bartender listened. We could now hear the shrieking of sirens and, I thought, distant shouts. The bartender said, "Sounds near. Bomb squad is on the way. I'm going to see," and ran out of the bar.

I waited for the inspector and thought of George Hobson. I had a great respect for seedy, evasive, loyal, honest—and murdered George Hobson. I wished, though that I knew whatever it was he was so determined not to tell me and yet felt that someone, Mr. Lowry, should know.

Dino—I was now sure, alive—was almost a smiling presence beside me.

I had never hated Dino. Once I believed myself in love with him and had been absurdly proud because with all his charm and good looks and attractiveness he had chosen me. I don't think that I was a gawky child; Aunt Loe had seen it that I had dancing and riding lessons. But I was certainly shy, chubby, red-cheeked and overclothed in tweeds and stockings and pullovers when I first met Mr. Lowry and Dino.

I had had a rather odd childhood, spent mainly under Aunt Loe's care in England; I had gone to a girls' school there and had been stuffed with potatoes, oatmeal and rules of conduct. When I was sixteen, it was decided that I should go to school in America; I was an American and Aunt Loe said it was wrong to bring me up in another country. She chose the school in Sampler Village, which was near the Lowry place, and enlisted Mr. Lowry's aid as a sort of godfather and guardian. At one time, which seemed to me then must be ages back in the past, Mr. Lowry had been an admirer of Aunt Loe's before she married and went to England to live. With Aunt Loe it was "once an admirer, always an admirer" and she had no hesitation about asking Mr. Lowry to look after me. Mr. Lowry immediately came to see me; he invited me to spend Christmas, which I had dreaded, at his home.

So began the strong affection I had for Mr. Lowry. He was kind, he was gentle, he gave me infinite understanding; he made me feel at home in the rambling Lowry house with its many fireplaces; he entered quietly into a corner of my heart which had been vacant; as time went on I found that I could bring him all my little problems and he considered them soberly and widely. Later, of course, after Dino had disappeared, he gave me a home; he would have turned over every penny of his much-depleted income to me if I had permitted it; I was given food, clothing, shelter and a father's warm care. He couldn't do enough for me.

That first Christmas I met Dino. He was probably the first boy—or young man—to invite me to a dance; he was certainly the first young man who ever kissed me. And his trips to Hong Kong the following year made him seem even more glamorous.

I was no younger than my classmates in school; somehow they seemed not older exactly, but more knowledgeable about the world, one another and young men. Their easy and graceful give-and-take only turned me silent and awkward. But I learned. All the girls had beautiful figures; I set myself to slimming down and it was not long before I induced Aunt Loe to let me choose my own clothes, rather than send them to me. She was alarmed by my measurements by then, but I assured her that slimness was chic. She wrote to me, rather wistfully, saying that clearly I was no longer in the puppy-fat stage and would soon be a young lady and she must somehow see to it that I was brought out, if she could scrape up some money, so we'd have to plan for my return to England. This terrified me; by that time Dino had come back from Hong Kong. I refused to leave America.

But it was really Mr. Lowry who married Dino to me; I didn't know it at the time. I was only awed, thunderstruck, proud because Dino asked me to marry him. No nonsense about going back to England. No worry about money; I had none except what Aunt Loe sent me (and I was uneasily sure she pinched her naturally extravagant purse to do so), but money didn't matter, Dino said; his father approved of me, his father would see to it that he had a good job. He was a little hazy about his job. I was in cloudland. We were married.

I don't think that Aunt Loe could have stopped it; I was determined. But I think that she might have made some suitable inquiries, she might have counseled time, a longer engagement, something, but she was ill with one of her prolonged sieges of asthma attacks. She could only rely on my own common sense, which had fled, and her long friendship with Mr.

Lowry. Mr. Lowry might have stopped it, but a father's patience and hope die hard. Later I understood perfectly why my father-in-law had desired this marriage. "But at the time I thought it was the right thing," he admitted once. "I thought Dino needed only to mature. I thought you were the right wife for him."

"You couldn't have stopped me," I told him and that was true, too. The marriage could, in fact, never have been a long one. We were living with Mr. Lowry when the final explosion occurred. And then Dino disappeared.

During the winter just past, Richard Blake had come back into my life. I had known him when I first knew Dino but only as one of a number of young men whom I met casually when Mr. Lowry or Dino took me to dances at the little country club, or when Mr. Lowry arranged Christmas or New Year parties at the big old Lowry house. I had liked Richard, but my eyes were dazzled by Dino; in literal fact I could see nobody but Dino. Richard left college, did his army service, came back and finished law school. I scarcely saw him during that time, although I heard of him now and then from his mother, our neighbor. I knew that he had graduated and was working as a junior member in the legal department of a big industrial firm, North Continent.

But at the previous Christmas Richard had come to spend the holidays with his mother. He had come to call on Mr. Lowry.

I suppose, if it hadn't been for Richard, and lacking any news of Dino, I'd have gone on for years, living quietly in the old and now shabby Lowry place, helping Mrs. Clurg see to the house and see to Mr. Lowry, playing endless games of chess with him, taking him for rides in his incredibly ancient but once-splendid Rolls-Royce and hoping it would hold together till we got home, hoping the leak in the roof was not a serious one, hoping that the three-hundred-year-old ash at the foot of the rather weedy garden would not need a tree surgeon. There would probably have been years of all these domestic chores, years of interesting myself in village affairs, the September Fair, the Red Cross Drive, the Christmas Sing. It was a busy enough life, though, for Mr. Lowry felt that my marriage had checked my education and undertook to complete it himself. He was an erratic yet entertaining teacher. He said of himself, quite truly, that he knew a little about a great many things. So we might dash from Latin verbs to Victorian history; he never liked Queen Victoria and gave me long lectures about China and the opium wars. He then might shoot off into the Marquise de Sévigné's letters. He also had a great affection for nineteenth-century English poets, especially Browning. I never knew what the next hour's agendum might be; I could only do my best to try to keep up with him and never quite succeeded.

And then Richard came and I was no schoolgirl.

Richard knew the situation for what it was. Without talking of it at all, we waited, and for a while we were content to wait. But then, inevitably, we were not content to wait.

Richard talked to other lawyers. The alternatives were clear: if Dino was alive I was still his wife; if dead, his widow; so the only way out was a clear-cut divorce on the grounds of desertion. Definite arrangements got themselves made. Aunt Loe read between lines and realistically sent me a little money so I need not take money from Mr. Lowry or Richard. She also told me not to be a fool about Dino's or about Mr. Lowry's feelings.

Suddenly the flicker of motion in the mirror behind the bar caught my eyes. I looked and then stared and didn't believe it but jumped up and whirled around, and Richard came walking deliberately into the bar and deliberately took me in his arms and said, "I came to get you." At the same time I said, "Oh, take me home!"

FIVE

After a while he put me back down in the chair at the table, said, "Where's the bartender?" and went behind the counter while I explained about the bomb.

"Oh, yes, I was in a taxi. It went off in the next street." Richard hunted around among the bottles and poured himself a gin and tonic. "Does that sort of thing happen often here?"

"No. At least I don't think so." I thought of the practiced way in which the inspector had shot out of the bar and the bartender had ducked behind the counter. "I'm not sure."

Richard came back, sat down opposite me and suddenly, wholeheartedly grinned. "You're a sweetheart and I love you." Then he gave me a searching look. "What's wrong?"

"The inspector will come back. He went to see about the bomb. Richard, I think Dino is alive but I don't know where he is and couldn't find Mr. Chen because he's dead but George Hobson, the man in the shop, was murdered—I found him—"

Richard put down his glass with a rattle. "*What are you talking about?*"

I told him rapidly, afraid that the inspector would return at any instant. I got George Hobson's note and the list of names out of my handbag and put them on the table for Richard to look at; I talked and talked and then could not possibly describe little old-young George Hobson, whose throat had been so neatly, so horribly and so very recently cut before I entered the curio shop that morning.

He put his hand, warm and strong, over mine. "Don't think about it. When you get down to the facts, you yourself can't have been the cause of his murder. What are you drinking?"

"I don't know. Oh, yes—brandy and soda—" I didn't quite trust my self-control and indeed I felt miserably unsteady all over again, as I had been in the curio shop. He went to the bar; he came back, put down another brandy and soda and said absently, "Don't drink it too fast. You're not used to

31

strong drink at this hour of the day." He sat down again and studied George Hobson's note and George Hobson's list.

I drank and looked at him and admired his tanned face and rather mussed-up black hair. He didn't have Dino's striking handsomeness, almost beauty; he had just a good-looking, plain young face, very thoughtful just then, and I thought I had never seen anything so attractive in my life. I could have cried and I could have purred, and as it was I sat there admiring. I also felt sure that everything, now that he had come, would be cleared up.

I was in for disillusionment about that, for when I said at last, "What are we going to do?" Richard gave me the most baffling answer a man can give a woman.

"I don't know."

I didn't say flippantly, That makes two of us. Presently he looked up. "You believe that Dino is alive?"

"I think so."

He nodded. "Seems logical. Yet the police know nothing about him."

"Nobody knows anything about him, I told you, except possibly—almost certainly George Hobson. I wish I hadn't questioned him."

"You had to," Richard said briskly, cutting off my useless remorse. "Nothing else you could have done. Well, there seem to be some questions here. Of course this list must be important. It has struck you that every city on it is a port?"

"I—well, no." I thought it over. "Chicago?"

"Look at a map sometime, dearie. The St. Lawrence Seaway."

"Oh. But there are no street addresses."

He shrugged. For a second I gave a slight inner salute to the conservative, good lines of American tailoring. His gray summer worsted was so welcome a sight that I could have patted his arm merely for the pleasure of touching his sleeve. But I wanted to touch the arm below it too.

Richard said, "Of course we can't send this to Mr. Lowry. He can't possibly do anything about it."

"Suppose he knows something about this list—what it means."

He considered that and finally shook his head. "I have never seen such an anonymous list of names in my life. It must be on purpose. Chosen aliases or a code. Everybody knows a John Smith or a Herbert Jones or—no, the problem is particular, the special—John Smith—who almost certainly is not a real John Smith. I can't make out anything of the numbers and letters that follow them, either. These also could be a code. If so, we have no key to it, unless Hobson's letter—" He broke off to read it again. "If there's a suggested code source, I can't find it. No, let's wait a while before we talk to Mr. Lowry. I'm going to take you home, you know. That's why I came. I couldn't stand it any longer."

Tears came to my eyes. I blinked them away and said practically, "I had already decided to go home. I have a reservation. But—if Dino is in Hong Kong we can't leave."

"What is your reservation?"

I got out my ticket and told him. I listened while he went to the bar again, found a telephone and after a little discussion got us both on the same flight.

He came back to the table. "Why do you want to find Dino?"

Why, indeed. "I just have to."

He waited a moment. "All right, tell me the truth. Do you have any lingering affection for him?"

"No!"

He was suddenly, perfectly ruthless. "Do you think he may have changed? Do you think of trying to make a go of your marriage again?"

"No."

"That's what Mr. Lowry wants."

"Yes."

Again he waited a moment, then he said quietly and really very gently, "I'm sorry for Mr. Lowry. But I don't propose to let my wife—or my life—be governed by sentiment about Mr. Lowry."

"Oh, Dick, it's not that entirely. I can't explain it but—well, I did promise for richer for poorer, in sickness and in health —oh, I only know that I have to find Dino and be sure that he is all right and—and get him back to Mr. Lowry if I can."

He looked down at the list. I couldn't read anything at all in his suddenly rather stony face. "The simple and sensible thing to do is turn this letter and list over to the police, go home, forget the whole thing and go on with our plans."

I said almost in a whisper, "If Dino is involved in something terrible, in murder or whatever it is that is dangerous, I have to stop him."

It seemed to me that gradually the stony look left his face, although his lips tightened. Finally he straightened up and said briskly, "All right. I guess I understand. Anyway, I'll try to help you. I don't think there is any point in our staying in Hong Kong in the hope of finding Dino. I can't believe that Dino could stay here long without someone of the British or American colony knowing about it. There's an excellent police force. They keep a tight check on visitors coming into Hong Kong. He might have managed to get into the city secretly but—no, we could stay here until doomsday and never find him. There's only one thing I see to do. When we land in San Francisco you'll go home. I'll work on this list."

"The man in San Francisco? What's his name—" I leaned over to look at the perfectly anonymous list. "John Smith of San Francisco. Really, Dick you *can't*—"

"It's the only kind of lead we have which may concern Dino."

"Do you mean that you are going from city to city, every city on that list, and try to find a special John Smith, a special Herbert Jones?"

"It may not come to that. If I had some notion of what these numbers and letters mean . . . I was never much for cryptography. Perhaps I can get somebody to work on them. It must be something very simple though. Well, I suppose it needn't be simple but I feel that it is. Now, Hobson says that someone was listening. Who?"

"Somebody was at the door. The man who took me there called him a beatnik type—long hair, fancy kind of dress."

"It doesn't sound like Dino. How about the shop? Could anybody have been in it without being seen?"

"There was a screen across the end of it. I suppose someone could have been behind it. I didn't see anybody. But Hobson was uneasy. He all but threw me out. He wouldn't talk. So somebody was close enough to hear him."

He thought that over. Then he looked straight at me. "You didn't tell the inspector who was talking to you, anything about Hobson's letter or this list. You're afraid that Dino is involved in something shady. Sometime somebody is going to let Dino take the consequences for whatever he does. Well—never mind, perhaps you were right. In any event, we'll have to go on the theory that Dino is alive, that somebody wants to stop your inquiries about him and—" He stopped and thought and then said flatly, "And that's all."

He looked up as the bartender came back, his white apron flapping. Richard said, "I helped myself. A gin and tonic, and a brandy and soda for Mrs. Lowry."

"Like another, sir?"

"I don't think so now. We might have the check."

"Yes, sir. I went out to see what 'appened. 'Orrible things, bombs. Not like the old days 'ere. Sometimes I think about going 'ome. But me family is 'ere. And we'll get things straightened out—thank you, sir." He took the money and the tip Richard gave him and looked up. "Oh, 'ere's the inspector back again. Wot'll you 'ave, sir?"

"Nothing, thank you." The inspector it was, apparently unruffled, apparently unconscious of the fact that his sun helmet had disappeared and that there was a reddish smudge across one beige-trousered leg. Richard had risen; the Hobson letter and list had vanished smoothly into one of his pockets. The inspector gave Richard an inquiring look and I introduced them—one-sidedly, since I did not know the inspector's name. He supplied it. "Inspector Filladon," he said and the two men shook hands. I had a swift impression that they were instantly prepared to like each other. Richard invited him to sit down and the inspector said he had to get back on the job. "We've been a little occupied recently," he said rather wryly.

"You're still here, though," Richard said.

"Ah, well, it's home to many of us. Things will straighten out," he said, as the bartender had said. Then he gave Richard a very straight, pale look. "I didn't know that Mrs. Lowry had a friend in Hong Kong."

"I just arrived," Richard said. "I came to take her home. We have reservations on a flight today." There was something both determined and tentative about his voice. The inspector sat down, then linked bony but well-kept hands together and thought for a moment, his icy eyes very sharp. Finally he said agreeably that he didn't see why we shouldn't leave as we had planned.

"I don't think we need detain Mrs. Lowry for an inquest and investigation," he said. "It seems quite unnecessary in these circumstances. We have the clear evidence that she came upon the murdered man by accident. No, I think you can go home as you have planned, Mrs. Lowry. I'll have to ask you to come around to my office and make a statement. For the record, as you Americans say. We'll take your address in the event that we need to reach you at any time. Or if"—he looked very straight at his hands—"by any chance we hear anything of your husband."

There was a little silence. Then Richard made up his mind, gave me an apologetic look but said firmly, "You do understand, Inspector, that—well, that this piece of jade Mrs. Lowry has told you about does suggest that somebody—the murdered man or somebody with access to the shop—knows something of Mrs. Lowry's husband."

The inspector looked up at Richard with another flash of approval. "Oh, yes. There could be some connection there." He obviously respected Richard for not having evaded that. He added promptly, "And I assure you that we'll look into it. But if Mr. Lowry—Daniel Lowry, didn't you say?"

I nodded; Richard nodded. The inspector went on, "I suppose it is possible that he has been in Hong Kong recently, but since Mrs. Lowry has already made inquiries about him which came to nothing, I think it likely that he has not been here at all since he disappeared."

Richard looked polite but doubtful. "Aren't there ways to get into the city secretly? From—well, even from China?"

The inspector sighed and looked at his hands again. "I expect there are always ways to do almost anything," he said wearily. "I didn't ask you, Mrs. Lowry, if you or your father-in-law had communicated with Interpol about this. We are members, you know. So are you Americans."

I thought back to the months when we first realized that Dino had disappeared, when we first made inquiries, when we first began to make use of every channel of information. "Oh, yes. I expect Mr. Lowry's inquiry is still in their files. Nothing came of it."

He gave a very small but very tired sigh, and rose. "This will take only a few minutes."

He glanced around, as if looking for his sun helmet, said absently that he had got into a little scuffle with some young troublemakers in the street and we went to his office. I made a detailed statement; I signed it; he made a note of my address.

It was not ended, however. He shook hands with me, looked at me earnestly with those pale, observant eyes and said that if I had any news at all of my husband he hoped I would let him know.

"It may be—very likely it is a fact—that nothing concerning your husband had anything to do with the murder this morning," he said. "All the same we'll have to make sure just what did happen, and if in the course of the investigation we do find there's some connection with your husband—well, we'll cross that bridge when we come to it. It may be some time, months even, before we can close the investigation." He looked very tired again and added, "Perhaps never. But usually we get these things straightened out."

He meant "get the murderer."

Richard said, "If Dino—that is, Daniel Lowry—should be in Hong Kong—"

Inspector Filladon picked him up immediately, "Oh, yes, naturally, we'll look out for him. Or any connection . . ." He left that sentence hanging in the air and shook hands with me again, which was practically effusive for an Englishman but which gave me a notion that he felt sorry for me. So I knew he intended to instigate a very thorough search for Dino, as well as a very thorough investigation into George Hobson's murder and the possibility that the jade piece and my inquiries about Dino had something to do with it. I might just as well have told him the whole story, I thought coldly.

He shook hands with Richard, who said, "Thank you. That is—well, if you need either of us or anything . . ." For a moment I thought that he had changed his mind and intended to give Inspector Filladon the list and the letter. He didn't and the inspector thanked us both again.

"He knew we didn't tell him everything," Richard said in the taxi on the way back to the hotel.

"But he let us go home."

"The world's a very small place. He knows he can get us back again any time he wants to. But I'll tell you this: if I were another kind of lawyer, not corporation but with a private practice of my own, and if I had a client who did what I've just done and what you've just done, I'd tell him he was a damn fool."

"Please, Dick—"

"Oh, I promised to string along with you. But I think it's all wrong."

"Dick, you're so—so reasonable and logical and you expect other people to go by rules. They don't."

"You don't," he said crossly but also with a reassuring hand over mine. "Well, we're committed to this course now. But this isn't the end of it with Inspector Filladon. He's going to do his best to find Dino or anything at all that concerns Dino. Well, he's right. Here's the hotel. We'd better have lunch."

So we had a late lunch which I thought at first I couldn't eat, but then suddenly felt very empty and hungry and did eat.

I was still surprised in a way because I had been permitted to leave, but Richard said absently that he thought one reason was because the inspector was only too glad to get me off his hands. "The police have their problems, obviously. An unattended and attractive young female"—Richard grinned and scooped up some soup—"is an additional problem. They like tourists but I doubt that they are really enamored of single lady tourists whom they have to look after. It's a lucky thing that the man from Dayton came directly after you into the curio shop. Mr. Dayton Ohio gave you a good firm alibi."

"Alibi!"

"Well, I don't think that anyone supposed for a moment that you killed Hobson; still, an alibi is a useful thing. But Filladon strikes me as a man with his full share of tenacity. And intelligence."

I felt that, too; I liked but I was also a little afraid of Inspector Filladon. Richard said after a moment, more cheerfully, "But I'm perfectly sure that he'll do far more than we could ever do about finding Dino, if in fact he is in Hong Kong. There's nothing we could do but wait—and ramble the streets and search. No future in that. We can't find Dino if he doesn't want to be found. We'll have to try the list."

It was suddenly time for us to leave and I went up to my room to pack the last-minute toothbrush and book, and surprised a maid rummaging my open suitcase.

SIX

She heard me close the door, whirled around and dropped a nightgown. She swooped it up, shoved it in the suitcase and said, "I'm so sorry, madam. I was very clumsy. I knocked your suitcase to the floor and everything fell out. I hope I have replaced things properly." With which she closed the suitcase with a shove of one rather plump but lithe hand, pushed down the locks with a remarkably broad thumb, too short and too thick for the rest of her hand, and drew back into the shadow of the window curtain.

So what was I to do? I debated briefly. She wore a red uniform which for an ugly flash made me think of the red silk where George Hobson had pillowed his head. She wore a proper white apron, white cuffs, white collar. Her dark hair was arranged in a very bouffant coiffure and her face seemed vaguely Chinese, Indian, Eurasian—I couldn't tell what. Her enormous spectacles obscured her eyes. She spoke clear and not uneducated English. I had an impression of a rather plump attractiveness.

I was sure that I had closed my suitcase before I went to the curio shop—or was I so sure? I had been intent upon George Hobson's letter and my imminent visit to the shop; I could not remember with certainty.

It then occurred to me, thinking of little George Hobson, that I myself would certainly have been in the unhappy position of a suspect, at least for a time, only that morning if the tourist from Dayton hadn't entered the curio shop practically on my heels. So I decided to accept the woman's story, but as a matter of fact not entirely, for I went to the suitcase, opened it and took a quick look through it. Nothing seemed to be missing, and I turned to reach for the telephone and call for a bellboy to carry down my suitcase and then discovered that if nothing had been missing from my suitcase, the maid in her proper maid's uniform was certainly missing, for she had quite simply and quietly vanished.

That was reasonable, however. She might have expected me to make some kind of scene, telephone for the manager, anything. Probably she had merely gone on about her duties. There was something, something very small, something very faint in the room which had barely impressed itself upon me, when the bellboy appeared. He was young, Chinese and dapperly uniformed. In the elevator the faint, small something in the room seemed to claim identity; just possibly it was some kind of perfume. I had thought there was a lingering trace of Chanel Number Five in George Hobson's shop.

It was preposterous to link a maid in the hotel with George Hobson's shop. Chanel Number Five is one of the most popular perfumes in the world of women. Richard was waiting for me in the lobby. I paid my bill, signing some of the traveler's checks with which Mr. Lowry had provided me, and wondered as I had wondered before then what securities of his modest remainder he had sold, or what beautiful remaining piece of Chinese art, in order to supply me with the thick sheaf of checks. I did not think of the maid in red again until I was in San Francisco—in the Jade Room at Gump's, to be precise.

It is both a long and a short flight from Hong Kong to San Francisco. We catch up on one whole day and that is to me a little disconcerting. There was not much chance for Richard and me to talk as freely as we would have liked; the jets were very silent and the plane was full of ears that could not help listening. Our stops in Tokyo and Honolulu were very brief, only an hour or so in each; we did not leave the airports.

And what we might have said would merely have been conjecture. The numerals and letters must indicate some sort of address, Richard said, some means of secret communication between the remarkably anonymous names on the list. This alone suggested an illegal enterprise. While pacing up and down at the airport in Tokyo, trying to get a little exercise, Richard came up with an odd suggestion. "I don't think Dino could possibly be involved in any sort of espionage. He's not the type."

In a way he put it charitably. The fact was that anyone who relied upon Dino for information, facts, accuracy or, unfortunately, mere truth made a serious mistake. Besides, even the most odious or surreptitious kind of espionage undoubtedly requires a certain amount of, say, courage.

But then, as Mr. Lowry had said, Dino might have changed.

Richard said, "No, I think we can dismiss that. But I wish I could get the hang of these numerals and letters."

We went back to the waiting plane.

At the Honolulu stop we debated again over handing the list to Mr. Lowry as George Hobson had told me to do. Again we decided to wait. "We can only do what seems to be the thing to do at the time," Richard said. "But you're to go straight home from San Francisco."

I said no, I wouldn't. He was too tired by then to argue and our plane was called. Richard was probably half drugged by weariness after two long plane trips; in any event, he made no objection when we reached San Francisco and I did not go on to New York. He only asked if I preferred any special hotel and then said it didn't matter, for it would be a question of getting reservations. He used the telephone and I waited until he came back and told the taxi driver that we were going to the Mark Hopkins.

The balmy, moist air of the Bay City revived us both a little. We had coffee in the dining room of the hotel and on the way Richard stopped to send a telegram. Once we were seated he told me why. "If the letters and numerals are a code, we can't get anywhere. I puzzled over them all the way here. There is a vowel count that cryptologists work on. I tried it in an amateur way. I really don't think there's a code. If there had been, Hobson would have been likely to give you some hint about it and he didn't. Mr. Lowry just might know something about it. I think I can find out whether he does or not without telling him the whole story. That can wait. The point is, if it's not a code, then it must be some easy way of getting in touch with John Smith and the others, whoever they really are. The letters and numerals may refer to street addresses or offices. The simplest thing I can think of is post-office boxes."

"The telegram you sent—"

He nodded. "I'll lurk in the post office, near that box number, if there is one, in the hope that somebody turns up. I'll try the main post office first. Seems likeliest—if I'm right. Don't hope for much. It's a pretty thin thread."

I started to put on my gloves but he stopped me. "No point in your lurking too. Try to get some rest. I'll see you later."

So by taking one almost ominously quiet step at a time, our course was actually decided.

I knew, and so did Richard, that he could lurk for days or weeks or months within a huge city post office and discover no John Smith, even if by some chance he were right about the mélange of letters and numerals which followed each name on the Hobson list. It was not likely that Richard's first try and first interpretation of the enigmatic letters and numerals could be the right one. Actually, I felt so thoroughly pessimistic that after a hot bath and a futile attempt to sleep, I decided to see something of the city at least and thus went to Gump's.

I was a stranger to San Francisco; I fell in love with the city that day. But it was Mr. Lowry who had talked to me of San Francisco and it was Mr. Lowry, I'm sure, who had told me that Gump's had a magnificent, indeed a unique collection of jade. I did not hope to find another near-duplicate of the piece that had been sent to Mr. Lowry; even if I had, it couldn't have been very enlightening. Mainly I simply wanted some place to go, something to do, and naturally the two pieces had aroused my interest in jade. However, probably everybody who visits San Francisco visits Gump's.

So I took a taxi which hurtled down Nob Hill at such a fearsome pace that I clutched the seat and braced myself. The taxi driver spotted me for a visitor the second time we stopped with full brakes at a street crossing and I gave a yelp. He advised me to go to Fisherman's Wharf for dinner and to be sure to see the old St. Francis bar. He would have continued, but just then we drew up at Gump's and I got out, shaken and thankful.

I did have a vague impression that a second taxi stopped just behind mine, and as I went into the store I had an even fainter impression that someone entered the store a step or two behind me. I happened to glance toward the door while I waited for a salesman and merely noted a woman standing with her back to me, a plumpish woman with an enormous coiffure of blond hair; she wore a black raincoat, and one black glove lay on a counter. The salesman then approached me and I asked if I could see the Jade Room.

Gump's was quiet and elegant; the young man who took me to the Jade Room could not have been more polite or, as a matter of fact, more impressive, for he gave me a short but apparently authoritative history of jade. He talked of jadeite; he talked of nephrite; he showed me ancient pieces. We were halfway around the room and I was goggle-eyed over a cabochon of gem jade which was so green, so cool, yet so full of being, so to speak, that I could scarcely believe it was not alive, when I became aware that the young man had glanced over my shoulder several times in a rather puzzled way.

He caught the question in my eyes and said, apologetically, "Someone—I expect you were intending to meet a friend here . . ."

"Why, no!" I whirled around in time to see a figure in a black raincoat vanish beyond the doorway. I turned back to the salesman. He said in an embarrassed way, "The lady seemed to be taking such an interest. Watching you. I mean —I thought perhaps you had an appointment with her—that is, a friend." He bogged down completely but gave another puzzled glance over my shoulder which somehow suggested that the interest of the black-raincoated woman had been unusually intent. So my memory flickered back to the taxi which had drawn up immediately behind me, to the woman with the blond hair and the black raincoat and black gloves who, I had idly thought, had entered the store a few seconds after I entered it but whose face I had not seen. Probably the mere fact that she was plumpish and I could not see her face reminded me of the maid in the red uniform in Hong Kong.

I looked again, too, but the doorway was blank and two women, dressed in the smart suits that the chic ladies of San Francisco wear (for the weather can change or a fog sweep in from the ocean at any moment), came into the room to look for Mandarin buckles, set with a knife and a pair of scissors; they were looking for a wedding gift. I thought of the curio shop in Hong Kong. The salesman directed them and began to talk of jade again. "You remember the old story of jade," he said and when I obviously remembered no old story about jade, he told me. "A young man was sent by his father to an elderly, very knowledgeable Chinese to learn jade. The first day he came, the old Chinese put a small object in his hands and then merely chatted for an hour and sent the young man away. The same thing happened the next day and the next and the next. After the same routine had gone on for some time, suddenly when the Chinese put a small object in the young man's hands, the young man cried, 'This is not jade!' Interesting, isn't it?"

I said yes, it was, and rather sententiously quoted Mr. Lowry: "'Like acquiring taste in anything. They say you can never understand music until you listen, listen, listen to Mozart. Appetite comes with eating.'" I then looked over my shoulder again but there was no black-raincoated figure anywhere.

When I described the piece of jade that Mr. Lowry had received, the salesman took me to another part of the store and showed me some medallions; they were beautiful but not at all similar to Mr. Lowry's. He explained that they were pleasant but not particularly valuable jade, and when I asked, he said that the store's buyers had imported them before the trade from China was cut off. In that sense they were unique and certainly charming. There was no connection between them and George Hobson's curio shop but I had expected none.

I remembered another famed name in San Francisco and asked the salesman to direct me to Magnin's, which he did. I thanked him; he said it was a pleasure; we parted and I think both of us took a long look around for a woman in a black raincoat, for when I reached the door and glanced back he was standing on tiptoe, looking at the various shoppers all around very intently. It seemed to me that the black-raincoated woman must have made a rather disagreeable impression on him. She made a disagreeable impression on me, I need not say. I thought again, uneasily, of the red-uniformed maid in Hong Kong. Yet I did not see how she could possibly have transferred herself to San Francisco, discovered me, followed me in a taxi and trailed me around Gump's.

I walked over to Magnin's thinking of that and realized that, of course, she *could* have contrived to get to San Francisco; there are many flights from Hong Kong; nothing would be easier than to inquire for Mrs. Lowry at hotels until she found me. But if so, then why? Common sense told me the whole thing was sheer fantasy. Some shopper or tourist had merely happened to arrive within seconds of my arrival at Gump's, had merely been curious about the Jade Room and that was all. I stopped at an intersection to wait for the traffic light to change. A hand snaked out from the group around me and neatly opened my handbag.

SEVEN

I must have felt some slight tremor or motion, for I looked down exactly as a hand in a black kid glove withdrew. In the same instant the traffic light changed, people surged past me and across the street, and the owner of the black kid glove was lost completely.

Bag snatching or wallet snatching can happen anywhere. In New York I had accustomed myself to carrying my handbag with the loop over my wrist and my hand firmly clutching the bag.

There was nothing in my handbag that would have been of value to anybody. My passport and health certificates for reentry to the United States were in the zippered compartment, which was still closed. My wallet had only a few bills. My folder of traveler's checks would have obliged anyone to show identification in order to cash them, and besides, they were insured. But naturally I didn't like that snaky black-clad hand. The traffic light had turned red again, so I had to wait another moment or so, which seemed a long time, but nobody came near me.

I couldn't help thinking of the woman in the black raincoat and black gloves at Gump's; there was no real reason to believe it was the same woman. I decided to take a grip on myself, my nerves and my galloping suspicions. I crossed with the light to Magnin's, took a delighted look around its glamorous first floor, bought six pairs of stockings (which later proved to be a good idea), then wandered out to the street again and past some shops which I vaguely remember, for all at once I found myself riveted before the window of a hairdressing salon. It was full of wigs.

Wigs of long hair, wigs of short hair, wigs of something which was not hair but looked like it, wigs of various colors, wigs.

The maid in Hong Kong had had an enormous coiffure of dark hair; I was sure of that. The woman in Gump's had an equally enormous mound of blond hair. Nothing would have been easier than for the brunette of Hong Kong to walk into a beauty shop and emerge as a blonde.

I told myself not to be a fool, and strolled back past Magnin's and across the street where there was a small park. By then people were streaming homeward; there were lines of cars and taxis passing. I sat for a while on a bench, immersing myself in the sights and sounds and atmosphere of San Francisco. The magical, mystical, romantic city entrapped me; I wanted to live there forever. I knew that someone sat down on the other end of my bench. I heard the rustle of a newspaper and barely glanced at a woman in a yellow coat. Mainly I was engrossed in savoring a kind of exhilaration, a zest in living which seems to come up from the sidewalks of San Francisco and hover in the air—which air all at once began to grow a little foggy and chill. The woman at the end of the bench had edged nearer me.

I must have felt her nearness, for I jerked around to look at her. She shifted her grip on the newspaper, she wore black kid gloves. Her newspaper was held up, so I did not see her face, but I did see her teased blond hair and had a glimpse of heavily rimmed glasses. She wore a yellow raincoat. She was almost within touching distance of me and my handbag.

I didn't wait for any further observation; I didn't wait for anything, but rose, walked rapidly back across the street, got a taxi almost at once and hurtled up Nob Hill again in a way which was almost as unnerving to me as my way down had been a little earlier.

Black kid gloves are nothing unusual; there had been a vogue for black kid gloves lined with silk. Perhaps she had merely found her end of the bench uncomfortable. I was in the elevator at the hotel before an odd thing presented itself to me, like a photograph: certainly her yellow raincoat had shown a black collar and a kind of black edge. Hadn't it?

That would mean, at least it *could* mean, that her coat was reversible. A black raincoat had slid very swiftly out of sight during my visit at Grump's. The pleasant salesman had believed that a woman was watching me. A black-gloved hand had certainly opened the catch of my handbag.

The sensible conclusion was that a purse snatcher had made an attempt to get hold of my wallet. I did not feel at all sensible. There was nothing in my handbag which could be of any value to anybody but me. Yet the Hobson letter and the Hobson list might have been expected to be in my handbag. Actually Richard still had them.

The strange world I had been introduced to when I entered the curio shop in Hong Kong asserted itself. In fact, however, the jade piece had opened the door to that world.

I was thankful to find a message from Richard. He had apparently shoved it under the door to my room. *"Maybe news, maybe not. Meet me Top of the Mark at seven. It's a cocktail lounge. The elevator boy will show you."*

"Maybe news, maybe not" was at least hopeful. I wished I had put my idle hours to better use, such as having my travel suit pressed. I brushed and brushed my hair (and simply could not keep from thinking of wigs), put on lipstick and a dab of luxurious scent which Aunt Loe had given me for Christmas and at seven o'clock found my way to the Top of the Mark, which was certainly not difficult, as the elevator was packed with others bent on the same destination. When I walked into the enormous lounge, the views on all sides took my breath away.

There were great plate-glass windows rising to the ceiling. Beyond them was sky and sea and a fantastic, graceful bridge and a whitish, barren-looking rock way out in the bay. On the other side there were mountains in blue and purple and gold. Tables filled the room and lined the windows. I couldn't move for a moment, and then Richard came, took my arm lightly and laughed. "Gets you like that, doesn't it? I've got a place over here so I can watch the elevators. If you want to look, that's the Golden Gate Bridge, right down there. Over there is Alcatraz . . ." A waiter was standing at his elbow. Richard ordered for both of us, took a nut from a dish on the table and said, "I think I found John Smith. Whether he'll turn up here or not is anybody's guess. He looked like a scared rabbit."

"Is he coming here?"

"I don't know. Short of clutching him by the arm and holding on till he yelled for the police, there was no way for me to make sure of him or anything. However, there was a box number that was the same as his number in the list. I couldn't quite believe it, but there it was and I found it. I could see a yellow envelope, which I thought was my telegram, through the little glass slit in the box. So there I stood, hanging around, leaning on a desk for postal orders and such, walking, roaming around until I was sure I'd be arrested for loitering. I went out once and got a sandwich but got back like a shot in case I'd miss him. About four o'clock my bird arrived."

He ate some more nuts.

"Go *on*. What happened?"

"Well, it got a little sticky right away. I watched while he opened the post-office box. Saw him take out my telegram. Saw him read it. I knew then he was my man."

He selected another nut and munched on it deliberately; I wished I could shake him. "What did he *do?*"

Richard seemed to consider it. "Looked sick," he said at last. "Like a heart attack, honestly. Absolutely purple and then ashy-white. I think I made a mistake."

"*What—*"

"Well, you see, if it did turn out that the number for John Smith was a post-office-box number—I really didn't think it was. I just couldn't think of any other meaning—anyway, if it did turn out that it was a box number and John Smith did turn up, I wanted to make sure that he was my man, so I pitched it strong. My telegram. A mistake, I can see now."

"*What did you say in the telegram?*"

"I said, 'INFORMATION HOBSON MURDERED ADVISE SEE MESSENGER.' "

I pulled the dish of nuts nearer and we both crunched for a while, thinking. "So he had a heart attack?" I said at last.

He glanced out at the incredible span of the Golden Gate Bridge and back at the elevators. "Not quite. But he was scared. I told you, I made a mistake. Anyway, I got him by the arm and he damn near jumped out of his skin. So I sort of hissed at him, conspiratorial, said he was to meet the messenger at the Top of the Mark and—" Richard got up. "Here he is."

Here he was and almost immediately he wasn't. I had only a glimpse of a fattish, baldish man in a brown suit who came out of an elevator, glanced around swiftly so his big spectacles winked, and as Richard sprang up, disappeared. He did disappear, exactly like that, into another elevator, the door of which was open. Richard ran after him; the next elevator door opened, Richard gave a kind of wave in my direction and then he too disappeared as that elevator went down. A group of men and women, together, talking and laughing, came into the lounge and I couldn't even see the elevators.

There was nothing to do but wait. However, considering the celerity with which Mr. Smith had disappeared I did not think Richard would overtake him, and he didn't. He came back in only ten minutes or so and sat down. "That's the end of that lead. I'll never see him again."

"Why did he run like that? Once he got here, I'd have expected him to talk to you."

"Oh, you didn't see? A woman came from somewhere and touched his arm. I think she said something. She vanished into the elevator with him. By the time I got into the lobby there was't a trace of either of them."

I had a kind of tingle, as if I knew what was coming next. "A blonde in a black raincoat?"

"A blonde. Yellow kind of coat. Didn't you see her?"

"Not then. Some people came out of an elevator. You were hurrying after John Smith. I couldn't see past you. But a woman in a black raincoat—except it could have been reversible and yellow on one side—anyway, she wore black kid gloves and she tried—I think she tried to take something from my handbag."

Richard gave me a long and very serious look. Then he ordered another drink and said, "You'd better tell me."

There was not much to tell, even though, making a thorough account of it, I also told him of the incident of the maid in Hong Kong, which no longer seemed trivial. "She was a brunette. The woman today was a blonde. It's very easy to buy a wig."

He turned and turned his glass, thinking. "It appears that somehow she knew in Hong Kong that you had the Hobson letter and list and followed you here. She must be a rather expert operator. It wouldn't be difficult to trace you; still, it takes some skill. If, of course, you're right and it's the same woman. Certainly that woman in the yellow coat got John Smith out of the way in a hurry. If she did follow you from Hong Kong . . ." He paused for a long time and finally said, "Then either she's been employed to get that letter and list back, or she has some more direct interest in whatever it is that George Hobson warned you was dangerous. No way to know about that. I blundered about John Smith."

"You were right about the post-office box."

"It was the only thing I could think of." He nodded at the waiter for the check and said, "Are you up to another plane trip tonight if I can get a reservation?"

He was far too casual and said "a" reservation, no plural about it. And no mistake about it, either. "You're not sending me home!"

"I can't leave you here alone with Blondie on the prowl."

"Where are you going?"

He gave me a half-amused, half-exasperated look. "I didn't

say I was going anywhere. Oh, all right. I'll try Herbert Jones in Tampa. Now then, I'll see if I can get you on a plane to New York."

"I'm going with you."

In the end he gave in again, probably for the same reason: he was simply too tired to argue. He said he gave in because I looked as if I were going to make a scene, and when I said I had never made a scene in my life he said darkly that you could never tell, and paid the waiter. We then went down to my room, where, after another debate about it, we decided to telephone Mr. Lowry and ask him only if he knew anything about the Hobson list. We weren't at all sure that it was the right thing to do. I put in the call and Richard stretched out on one of the beds and shut his eyes. Mr. Lowry himself answered. He was rather testy. "Time you phoned me. I tried to get you in Hong Kong and they said you'd left. So now you're in San Francisco . . . Any news of Dino?"

We had decided what I was to say, which was the literal truth. "Mr. Chen's dead. I couldn't find Dino. I think, though, that he's alive. I'll explain when I get home."

Mr. Lowry cleared his throat. "I see. Yes. Is he in trouble?"

"I don't know. I can't talk now."

"But I insist—oh, well, all right. Young Dick Blake catch up with you?"

"How did you—yes, he did. In Hong Kong."

"I talked to his mother," Mr. Lowry said. "I'll expect you home tomorrow."

"Not—not tomorrow."

His voice sharpened. "Why not?"

I shot a glance at Richard for help. He swung his legs around and took the telephone as Mr. Lowry said, "You're hiding something from me—something about Dino. You'd better tell me—"

By that time Richard had the receiver in his hand. "Hello, Mr. Lowry . . . Yes, I heard you . . . Well, we're not sure. We believe Dino is alive and we may have news of him. It's a long story—" Mr. Lowry's voice rumbled out angrily. Richard waited and then said, "Yes, quite, but not on the phone." He sounded as sharp and authoritative as Mr. Lowry, which must have given my father-in-law a shock, for nobody ever talked to him like that. "Just now," Richard said crisply. "I want to know whether you know any of these men. Have you got a pencil . . . all right, but you'll need one. John Smith of San Francisco—"

The telephone muttered and rumbled and kept on muttering and rumbling as Richard went down the list. I heard Mr. Lowry when it came to James Black, New York. "Good God!" he shouted indignantly. "I must know a hundred James Blacks! What *is* this?"

"I'll tell you when I get home," Richard said. "Marcia is going with me."

Mr. Lowry must have said something particularly explosive, for Richard said, calmly, "I'm sorry, sir. She's just gone out. I'll tell her what you said."

He managed to say good night politely before the telephone wire sizzled. Then he turned to me and said soberly, "Mr. Lowry is right, though. I ought to pack you off home."

We went to Tampa. Richard telephoned for reservations and there was a flight out in about four hours. Blondie went too, but not on the same plane.

EIGHT

We made sure of that. We were careful in a way which seemed absurd and childish and yet mandatory.

First, Richard made a copy of the Hobson list and put it in his wallet. We could have memorized the short list of names and cities; the jumble of letters and numerals would have been difficult to memorize accurately. He then put the original letter from George Hobson and the original list in an envelope, and addressed it to himself in care of his mother.

"The letter is the important thing," he said. "This is what anybody in his right mind would have turned over to Inspector Filladon. Well, for that matter, the list too. There must be some way of tracing these men."

"Dick, please don't start to argue again!"

He licked the envelope. "If it is evidence about Hobson's murder, and I think it is, we have no right to keep it."

"He didn't sign it. He didn't even write it—"

"He probably used some old typewriter in his shop. Nothing easier for the police than to trace the type."

"We have to try to find Dino first. You promised me."

"I was a damn fool. Have you got a stamp?"

I rummaged in my bag and found a little book of stamps, and watched, doubting my own decision and the decision I had all but forced upon Richard, while he stamped the envelope. I had begun to know Richard; he was reasonable and logical; he respected a sound and valid emotion; he despised phoniness. He was never impulsive; he was deliberate and thoughtful by nature.

He glanced up at me. "I can't help being the way I am," he said, as if reading my thoughts in my face. "I believe in the law. No body of laws can be perfect. No humans can be perfect. But the law tries. It is the only wall of protection for —for civilization," he ended up and suddenly grinned at me, put out a hand to push back my hair and then held me close to him. "It's all right. I'm not going to lose any sleep about all this. You're worth going against my good sense." He let me go. "I'll send this letter along to my mother and when, or if, the time comes, we'll hand it over to Filladon. Don't look so glum."

"Mr. Lowry will get it out of her. He'll ask her if she's heard and she'll tell him there is a letter addressed in your handwriting and he'll get it out of her."

"He wouldn't open it."

"You don't know Mr. Lowry!"

He thought that over and shrugged. "Do you have a scarf you can put over your hair?"

I dug out a green scarf and adjusted it over my head.

"You'll have a long wait at the airport. But I think you'd better start. We'll not go there together. No sense in letting Blondie spot you because I'm with you. She got a good look at me in the bar. Go quickly through the lobby—that is, not too quickly; don't make yourself conspicuous. Take a taxi, not the first taxi but the second." He grinned again. "Any school-child knows the routine. All the same, hide your hair and don't take the first taxi—" The telephone rang.

"It's Mr. Lowry," I said dismally.

Richard answered but it wasn't Mr. Lowry. He said, "Hello —hello . . . Oh, I see. That's all right." He put down the telephone looking rather odd. "Blondie, I should say. A woman's voice. Said she had rung the wrong number. Didn't expect a man to answer, obviously. Did the maid in Hong Kong have any special accent?"

"She spoke very clearly. I think there was just a slight British accent."

"Could be the same. If so, she is checking on you and your room. I only hope John Smith doesn't warn our man in Tampa. I'll stop at the desk and pay our bills. I'll bring your suitcase. Just go out and—be careful, Marcia."

I put my travel coat around me and took my handbag. He opened the door, glanced out at the corridor, said, "Coast seems to be clear," kissed me lightly and gave me a little shove.

I saw nobody at all in the corridor. There were only two passengers in the elevator, obviously a man and his wife, who talked about Trader Vic's all the way down to the lobby. I gathered that I had missed something by not having dinner there, and went out through the lobby without looking to right or left. I needn't have worried about taking the second cab because the elevator couple took the first cab and I took the second and reached the airport with only a few moments of panic at the downhill street crossings.

There I waited. I waited and waited. I didn't see anyone who remotely resembled Blondie. The happy conversation of the tourist couple in the elevator nagged at me; I wished there had been a chance for at least one splendid gourmet dinner in one of San Francisco's famous restaurants. I was so hungry that I risked going into the restaurant for a sandwich and coffee, but it was so brightly lighted that I was nervous and on edge, swallowed hurriedly and quickly went back to the inconspicuous corner behind a rank of telephone booths. There again I waited.

After what seemed to me an eon or two, our plane was called. If Richard had arrived I had not seen him. Certainly I had not seen Blondie. I slid out and went to the gate, quickly, feeling very furtive and looking for Blondie and for Richard. I stood at one side watching the passengers, and Blondie was not among them. At the last moment, though, Richard came running, carrying his bag and mine. We were in fact the last passengers on the plane.

As we ran he said quickly, "Sorry I was so late. It was Blondie, but she got away from me before I could choke the truth out of her."

We boarded the plane and the chance for much conversation of a really private nature was gone. We sat together but we might as well have been in different sections. As we were fastening our seat belts and there was a little stir and commotion in the plane, he told me that he had stayed a short while in my room, thinking he'd give me time to get away. As he waited somebody tried a key in the door of my room.

He thought at first it was a maid but the lock wouldn't move. He then went to the door and in a moment there was a kind of soft push and thrust and he thought he could see the very edge of a piece of celluloid. So he flung open the door but he was a fraction of a second too late, for Blondie, in her black raincoat and blond wig, if wig it was, was streaking down the corridor. She whirled around a corner, he after her, and by the time he had turned the corner, she had vanished. "Into a room, into a serving pantry—I couldn't guess where. I opened the door into a linen room. I looked down the fire escape. No Blondie anywhere. It was like John Smith's disappearance. It was like a vanishing trick. Whatever she is, Marcia, she's like a professional."

We soared up into the night sky. When we leveled out he

said, in almost a whisper and very crossly, "I'm a fine detective. I let John Smith get away. I let Blondie get away. We may be shooting off into the blue in more ways than one."

Almost before we knew it we had landed at Los Angeles and taken off again. Once more we were flying toward the sun, and dawn came so soon that I could scarcely believe it. I remember thinking of the long months it took for the prairie schooners and the hardships those early travelers had to go through.

There was a little turbulence over the Gulf, not much, and before it seemed at all possible we arrived at the wide-flung Tampa airport. I was beginning to feel that I had taken up permanent residence in vehicles shooting through the air at fantastic speeds and I was glad to get my feet on the ground.

Richard saw to it that I had my own suitcase and then left me on a bench while he disappeared toward some telephones. Nobody seemed at all interested in me. When he returned he looked both relieved and troubled. "They're gone," he said. There was a baggage truck heaped with suitcases near us and nothing else at all, yet he lowered his voice and spoke quickly. "A man I knew in the army. Gill Rayburn. He and his wife have a house near Tampa but they're on an island in the Keys. However, I got his phone number from the maid and talked to him and it's all right for you to stay there." He scribbled the address on a page from his pocket notebook. "Go there by taxi. Take your suitcase. The maid, Bessie, will be there to let you in."

"But—"

He cut me short. "Safer for you than a hotel. Nobody will know where you are.

"What about you?"

"I'll come along later. I'll try the main post office first, as I did in San Francisco. It's sure to be the largest one. If I can't find the number for Herbert Jones, I'll inquire about the branch post offices. It'll take time. Here's a porter." Richard nodded at me and went away. The porter carried my suitcase and found a taxi for me. Rather helplessly I gave the driver the address on the paper in my hand.

By this time I had lost my sense of hours of the day. I knew it was morning but that was about all I knew. It did strike me that the air was not only very hot but seemed remarkably still and oppressive. The driver said cheerfully, "Hurricane weather. Radio says there's one headed this way. Name's Edith." We stopped for a traffic light and the driver cocked his head to one side, listened and said, "Hear that?"

I heard the sound of motors around us; then from somewhere, from everywhere, it suddenly seemed to me there was a light sound of tapping, like a hundred woodpeckers vigorously at work. The driver must have seen my puzzled face in his mirror, for he chuckled, "People boarding up their windows. But don't be scared, miss; them hurricanes is likely to do anything. Edith may not get here at all—may hit down in the Caribbean, Central America, out over the Gulf, anywhere. Edith. My wife's name." He chuckled again, not too obscurely amused.

It proved to be a rather long taxi drive; the Rayburn house was in fact some distance from the city itself.

I don't remember that I had any reluctance to park myself at the Rayburn's house, but when we drew up at a white stucco wall with a tall gate, I instantly realized how much more pleasant their house might be than any hotel in the world. Their maid took my suitcase from the taxi driver and led me through the gate into a perfectly enchanting kind of patio or courtyard which proved to run halfway around the house, including the front entrance, doors to two bedrooms which stood out from the house like ells, and the back entrance. Everybody, it developed, used the front gate. There were glossy-leaved oleanders in the patio, and gardenias in bloom; there were camellias not in bloom then but crowding the paths; there was a little fountain trickling merrily upon a tiny pool full of purple and white water hyacinths; there was a gigantic tree hung with Spanish moss (the maid later told me it was an ancient water oak) and there were sprays of tiny white orchids clinging to the tree. It was a tropical garden; there were palm trees, bamboos, bougainvillea, and other growth I could not identify.

Bessie was middle-aged, large, smiling, spotlessly uniformed and warm in her welcome. Miz Rayburn had telephoned to her. She was to see to me—meals, everything. She ushered me into a charming guest room through the door directly from the patio. There was another door leading to a hall. She had opened the shutters; she showed me an adjoining bathroom which was so trim, so new and modern in its gay shocking pinks that I thought of the claw-legged bathtub in my bathroom at the Lowry place with a kind of surprise. Bessie ran the tub for me. She said that Miz Rayburn had said that there was a gentleman, Mr. Rayburn's friend, who would be staying there too and his room would be on the other side of the patio, but he wasn't expected until dinnertime. There was a pleased gleam in her eyes, as if she scented romance.

The obvious fact that Richard and I would be staying in his friend's house alone had not even seemed unusual to me until then. The fact was that I was only too glad that Richard would be there. Apparently the Rayburns had taken the thing quite in their stride, without any question; I instantly liked the Rayburns and I also liked the maid, who clearly felt that what Miz Rayburn said went, and that was all there was to it. While I was in the tub Bessie unpacked my suitcase and vanished, and my two dresses, my small supply of lingerie and wrinkled travel suit vanished too.

I thought of Richard and the post office and the very dubious success of his undertaking. After I got out of the tub I went into the patio in my dressing gown, leaned back in a green and white lounge chair and listened to the bubble of the fountain—and to the distant woodpecking.

I hadn't noted much of the street when I arrived in the taxi but the woodpecking did seem to be very far away. Presently I went to the tall gate, found that it was bolted, opened it and looked out. There was green everywhere up and down the street, which was paved but rather narrow with some kind of coarse grass pushing its way up wherever there was a slight crack. There were palm trees, some spiky shrubs I learned later were palmettos, and a general air of isolation which just then pleased me. I had a notion that perhaps the land was part of a development which hadn't thoroughly developed, so to speak. Perhaps it was too far from the city. There seemed to be a house on one side; I could see a low roof and thickly growing shrubs, but that was all. I dropped the bolt in place again; that suited me too and added to my sense of content.

Bessie brought me lunch and put it on a little table in the patio and when I spoke of the fountain she said yes, it was a regurgitating pump, which seemed a suitable enough word, although I believe the correct one is "recirculating." In any event, it was run by electricity and she showed me the tiny button which turned it on and off; the pleasant bubble stopped for a second, and then, as she pressed the button again, started up. Otherwise the patio, the house, the street, the whole world seemed remarkably still.

"I pressed that silk suit of yours," Bessie told me. "Pressed the yellow linen and the little black silk, too. They're in your room. Rest of the things I just rinsed out." She straightened a glass. "Miz Rayburn didn't know how long you'd be here. She just said I mustn't tell anybody. You might want to go to Maas Brothers and see can you get a thin dress or two. Weather's likely to be hot this time of the year."

We settled that I'd go to Maas Brothers, which I took correctly to be a large department store, the next day. I asked her if there was any news of the hurricane.

"That!" she said scornfully. "Don't you worry about any little old hurricane. Likely to go north or south or anywhere. I've seen them turn back on their own tails."

"People are boarding up windows."

"Oh, sure. Our windows here don't need it. All have shutters, good and strong. House good and strong and low. Wall protects it, too. We don't worry about hurricanes. And you don't worry about anybody finding you. I'll see to that. I wonder now what Mr. Blake likes for dinner."

There was a definitely romantic gleam in her eyes; it suggested that she took me and Richard to be an eloping couple, hotly pursued by detectives, irate husband, wife, or all of them. I said he'd like anything she cooked and was safe in saying so, for when he arrived by taxi, hot and tired, Bessie had a hot bath waiting for him, a pitcher of cold martinis and a broiled steak. Again he had had a certain amount of luck.

"It's the main post office this time, too," he told me, sipping a martini. "I didn't have to explore the branch post offices, for I did find the right number. I sent a telegram again. Hung around all afternoon; nobody came."

He looked around him. "Gil's done well for himself."

"I think Bessie thinks it's a love nest for us. Temporarily, anyway."

"Then she's all for it." He was reviving. "She practically apologized for putting me in the bedroom on the other side of the patio. She said pointedly that both rooms opened on the patio." He leaned back in the comfortable patio chair and took a long breath. "I could wish we were on a honeymoon. Maybe Gil will lend us this place sometime." But he sobered and so did I, for "sometime" seemed a long way off.

He was then unexpectedly overtaken by a spasm of conventionality and said that if I minded his staying at the house he'd go to a hotel, and I told him not to be ridiculous and I'm perfectly sure that neither of us could avoid thinking of the very short distance across the grassy paths of the patio, between fragrant gardenias and in the stillness of the tropical night. When Bessie announced dinner we walked holding hands as if we had been drawn together magnetically, all the way through a wide, airy hall and into a dining room with something pleasantly Spanish about the table and chairs, and a terrazzo marble floor.

Bessie drew curtains over already closed and shuttered windows. She lighted candles and said too encouragingly that she didn't "live in." She went home at night and she'd lock the back door and wouldn't return until time for our breakfast. It was so insinuating that Richard looked at me and I looked at him and laughter leaped between us, and romance was shattered for the moment, which really did seem too bad, I thought later, alone in the green and white and camellia-pink guest room, with the French doors open on the patio. When I turned off my lamp I could see Richard's light opposite, beyond the shadowy shapes of shrubbery. It was very quiet everywhere.

We hadn't talked much after dinner; we only sat again in the patio, in the soft darkness, drinking our coffee, and later Richard had gone into the house and poured himself a nightcap. He turned on a radio in passing and came out with the news that the hurricane had apparently halted over the sea somewhere near Cuba. He intended to follow the same pattern of post-office patrol the next day; he said that he didn't know what else to do. He hoped that this time he'd not be fool enough to let his man get away from him. He was not exactly optimistic and neither was I.

It was late, I suppose, before I could sleep, for when I awoke Richard had already had breakfast and was gone.

The sky was overcast and Bessie was slightly downcast when she brought me a papaya and coffee and, I suspected, noted that only one person had slept in the bed. When I asked her, she said that old hurricane was hanging around Cuba, couldn't make up its mind. She brought in a little heap of freshly washed lingerie, told me that all my stockings had runs in them and asked if Mr. Blake would be home for lunch. I said I didn't think so, and got out a pair of the stockings I had purchased in San Francisco—and had then gone to a bench where a woman sat down near me and stealthily edged nearer. After Bessie had gone and I was dressed I went out into the patio again. It was like an enchanted island of beauty and quiet. Indeed it was almost too quiet, that day.

The sky hung heavy and still. The remote sound of wood-pecking had diminished, so I thought everybody was waiting for further news of the hurricane before taking more steps of preparation for it. The air was so very still, so hot and humid that by noon my yellow dress was wrinkled and limp, as if I'd worn it for weeks. Bessie telephoned for a taxi, and I went to Maas Brothers. On the escalator, going up, I passed a woman going down who gave me a little shock, like a touch of electricity.

She had a rather thick-set but young figure, very large dark glasses and a quite flagrant wig that didn't even pretend to be hair but looked like the cotton candy I had been given as a child at the Village Fair. There was something about the shape of her face, something about her lithe yet plumpish figure that seemed familiar, and then we had passed each other. I couldn't tell whether she looked at me more closely than was comfortable or not. It seemed so, for I felt a kind of tingle of uneasiness. The cotton-candy wig was a bright, harsh yellow. I couldn't exactly hop over the dividing rail as I wanted to do; I had to wait until the escalator took its deliberate course up to the next floor. I then whirled around and took another deliberate way down again, but of course by the time I had got back to the first floor there was no Blondie—Goldie would now be more appropriate—in sight. Also, I wasn't at all sure that Goldie had been Blondie.

She could easily have guessed that the list would take us to Tampa in search of Herbert Jones. She could easily have followed us. Like me, she could have found herself in need of some cooler clothing.

Even if it had been Blondie, now Goldie, there was nothing much I could do about it then and there. There was in fact nothing Richard could do about it even if I got myself to the post office, found him and told him that I had thought— only thought—that there was something about a woman on an escalator which reminded me of Blondie. And of course the more I thought of it and the harder I tried to remember some detail, no matter how small, that had reminded me of her, the less likely it seemed to me that the woman was Blondie. In the end I went back up the escalator and bought some blue denim shorts and sneakers and two or three shirts. I couldn't get Blondie-Goldie entirely out of my mind, though. A woman had opened my handbag at a street crossing in San Francisco and then vanished. A woman had warned off John Smith. A woman had tried to get into my room in San Francisco and had vanished again when Richard tried to stop her. At last I put the dress box under my arm and left the store, and also left its bracing coolness; the heat and heaviness of the street fell upon me like a stifling sort of blanket. Perhaps I wanted to shake off the uneasy, indeed the frightening notion that I had seen Blondie; in any event, when I got a taxi I told the driver that I was a stranger to Tampa and that I'd like to see something of the city, so he took me first to a fishing wharf where smallish boats, laden with ardent fishermen, were coming back from the bay with triumphant strings of perfectly stupendous fish. Then he took me to the docks; Tampa was a port and an important one; there were ships, mainly cargo ships, from everywhere. We got close enough for me to see that it was a beehive of activity. San Francisco a port, Tampa a port, New York a port, Chicago a port; it was certainly an indication that whatever Dino was involved in had something to do with shipping, but that was all.

Tampa has climate and beauty but it is by no means a lazy resort city; the taxi driver took me through the busy streets, past industrial plants, past Tampa University, with its towered and verandaed one-time luxury hotel, now turned into classrooms. "Old Man Plant built it," said the taxi driver. "Place up the line called Plant City, too. He was a big shot one time here. Now you'd like to see Eboe City." He said "Eboe," like that, although I saw a sign which read "Ybor City." I couldn't understand the signs on the stores and restaurants because they were mainly in Spanish. The streets here were packed, too. "Cubans," said the driver, gesturing. "Spanish. Want to see a cigar factory?"

I said no, and he was disappointed. "Best cigars in the world."

By then it was late afternoon. I told him to take me to the Rayburn house. It seemed to me, as we at last approached the white wall with the sheltering high gate, that the palm trees along the road were swaying just a little, very gently, yet again rather ominously.

The gate was bolted, so I rang the bell. Bessie came running to open it. "Ma'am! There's somebody—he insisted—he pushed his way in!"

A man in a silk suit, which reminded me at once of Hong Kong, rose from a chaise longue behind Bessie. He came into full sight, sauntering along across the patio, handsome, smiling, with all his blue-eyed charm turned on. "Hello, darling," Dino said.

NINE

I remember that I dropped my dress box and Bessie's crisply starched uniform rustled as she picked it up. Bessie gave me a wild look. "Shall I send for the police?"

My heart really had stopped along with my breath and voice, for all at once it jumped and began to pound and my voice came back, although it was a husky kind of whisper. "No, Bessie. He's my husband."

Dino smiled and advanced toward me. Obviously Bessie's worst fears were confirmed; here was the irate husband discovering the eloping lovers, and she was on my side. "You get out of here, you," she said to Dino in such a way that it was really very menacing. "You got no right busting your way into this place. You got no business here."

I couldn't see more than the top of Dino's head, for Bessie was now between us, but I could hear him and I knew that he was a little taken aback. "My good woman," he said with forced amusement, "kindly get out of my way!"

"I don't take orders from you—" Bessie began, but I had to talk to Dino, so I said, "It's all right, Bessie. Really it's all right."

She waited a moment and then trudged toward the house, but at the door she looked back. "You call me, Miz Lowry, if you need me. I got me a good big broom in the kitchen. And I got a loud voice to yell with."

"Thank you, Bessie," I said and meant it, although Dino's blue eyes sparkled with sarcastic pleasure.

"Dear me, a dragon to protect you. Well, darling, aren't you glad to see me?"

He came toward me, the tall figure outlined with frightening distinctness against the glossy green shrubbery. He was fatter; there were plump pouches around his eyes, a soft roundness of his cheeks, and a little paunch with his Hong Kong-tailored suit did not disguise. He looked older somehow and far too well fed. He had let his wavy brown hair grow long and thick, almost to his shoulders; he wore a small but bushy beard. He looked, in fact, like an elderly beatnik and something stirred in the back of my mind, as if in a particular kind of recognition. I couldn't just then haul it out and identify it, for mainly I knew that if I had ever so much as toyed with the idea of Mr. Lowry's that Dino might have changed and that we could take up our marriage again, I had been a great fool. I could not bear his approach, his nearness, his apparent intention to take me in his arms and make a reunion of our meeting. I backed against some bougainvilleae, felt its flowers brush my hand and said, "Where have you been?"

"Darling," Dino smiled, his blue eyes at their most charming and luminous. "I should ask you some questions, shouldn't I? What are you doing here? And with our friend Dick Blake? Or should I say 'friend'? You are still my wife, you know."

I was not exactly in command of my wits. I grasped at the first question that came to me. "How did you know that Dick is here?"

"Why, your maid—somebody's maid—the virago with the broom in the kitchen told me."

"I don't believe you."

"Really, darling—"

"You've been following me!"

"Any reason why I shouldn't try to find my wife?"

I began to rally a little. "Your father—Dino, it's been so dreadful for him. We thought you were either dead or kidnapped!"

Something flickered in his eyes. I realized too late that I had provided him with an excuse for his disappearance and I was sure that presently he would employ that excuse. I said sharply, "You must phone your father at once."

His easy smile did not waver, his eyes didn't change. "My father wouldn't be at all interested in me. He turned me out, remember? He's a pompous old goat and if he's well rid of me, as he made it clear he hoped to be, I'm well rid of him. Has he got any money left at all?" The question was unbelievably callous, yet he wanted to know the answer. Dino was always interested in money.

"Your father gave you everything he could give you!" I said hotly. "You took what you could get. He kept you out of trouble—"

Dino waved one hand which had once been graceful and was now pudgy. "Spare me past history. Aren't you going to give me a welcome, darling? I am your husband. Your loving, faithful husband—"

I was really stunned by this. I think I said "faithful" with a kind of snort but he went smoothly on, "You were quite right. I—I was kidnapped. Very astute of you to guess it. I'd never have stayed away from you so long if I could have helped it."

Dino had two talents; one was for ladies and one was for lying. The ladies had to be a little naïve and unsophisticated, as I had been when we were married. The lies wouldn't convince a child in his senses, but they had once convinced me. Now I could almost see the gaudy wheels of his invention begin to spin. "I was kidnapped. It was really quite dreadful. It happened in . . . in Thailand. Near Bangkok. I had gone out to see a man, somebody who was supposed to make some fine designs for silk and I thought we might do a bit of business and . . . I came back at night, which was a mistake. I was driving a hired car. And these bandits simply stopped my car and . . . kidnapped me and I was helpless. Months on end—"

"They didn't think of asking for a ransom."

"Ransom? Oh—that is, why yes, they did. They said they had no answer. So they turned me over . . . to another band of kidnappers. And they—"

"Dino, stop lying. You disappeared because you wanted to."

"I'm telling you the truth. Listen to me, darling. I might stay away from my father, who hates my guts, anyway. But I would never stay away from you all this time if I could have helped it. Believe me—" He started toward me again and I pulled back. It was the kind of revulsion I might have felt for a spider. Mr. Lowry had been right in one way; Dino had changed—but not for the better.

He said, "You were always a cold little thing. Never mind, I'll soon see to that. Now we're back together again."

I wanted to run for the house and Bessie with her broom. I said, and I was ashamed to hear the unsteadiness in my voice, "Your father doesn't hate you. He sent me to Hong Kong to find you. He says—he says you are his son and he wants you back."

That stopped Dino for a moment. He gave me a blank, bright blue stare. Then he laughed. "You're lying now! My father told me he never wanted to see me again."

All at once I felt only very tired. "You can't blame him for that. He got job after job for you. Everywhere you did something dishonest, something wrong, something he had to make as right as he could. You bled him for money, Dino. And that last time at the brokerage firm—"

His eyes had taken on a queer kind of glaze, like that on porcelain but not as attractive. "Shut up," he said.

I was not afraid of Dino. "He made good on those bonds you managed to get away with. He gave you money to go out East. You said that all you wanted was a chance to start over again. You promised him—"

His mouth seemed to be shaped like a smile within that bushy small beard but it looked more like a snarl. "You were the one who searched out my checkbook, darling. I haven't forgotten that."

"I haven't forgotten what I found in it, either." But it was water over the dam, it was all in the past; I didn't care how many women Dino had kept in cheap little apartments in town, or what kind of women, or what he had done with the money he had induced his father to give him. The brokerage firm had let Dino off; I didn't know just how my father-in-law arranged it, but Dino was free. So he went out East; he disappeared because he wanted to. I asked, not caring much, "Why did you come back?"

"To my wife?" He asked in such fond tones that it was a blatant mockery. "Of course I came back. As soon as they got tired of keeping me and released me."

"How did you find me?"

Nothing was easier for Dino than to lie, quickly, with scarcely a thought. "I saw you. I—I took a cargo ship that was sailing for Tampa. It was a cheap passage; that's why I didn't fly home. In any event, I happened to see you on the street—" Even Dino seemed to realize that there was a hole in this, for he stopped and shoved the back of his pudgy hand over his long wavy hair, which didn't give him a look of youth at all, but was instead rather revolting.

"You came here, to this house," I said. "How did you know the address?"

Dino smiled smugly and triumphantly. "You never give me credit for intelligence, darling. The point is, I've found you. I'm staying here with you."

I sensed Bessie's bulky presence just inside the open front door. It gave me courage. "You are not staying here! But you are to phone to your father. *Now!*" I started toward the front door, Bessie, and the telephone that stood in the hall.

He put out a flabby hand and caught my wrist. "Just a minute, darling. You said you went to Hong Kong. Why?"

"Because Mr. Chen sent a piece of jade to your father. Your father thought that Mr. Chen had some news about you and that that was his way of letting him know."

The hand gripped hard; it was moist but not as flabby as it looked. "And did you talk to Chen?" Dino asked so slyly that I knew that he was perfectly aware of Mr. Chen's death.

"No. Let me go."

"Didn't you see anybody in Hong Kong?"

"Yes." I spoke too hastily. "I saw George Hobson."

Dino's eyes were very still. "George Hobson? I'm afraid that means nothing to me. Who is he? Did you talk to him? What about?" He paused a second and said, "Do go on, darling. I'm fascinated. Tell me all about this—this mysterious George Hobson."

It was too glib. I said, "He tried to warn your father. He knew—" I stopped, for all at once a palm tree above our heads and beyond the white wall gave a sharp rattle like a warning. I looked up; the sky had taken on an odd color, a kind of grayish yellow. The palm trees rattled again and the oleanders around us whispered. The clump of bamboos in the corner of the patio murmured and rustled together.

Everything then, abruptly, settled back at once into its heavy, waiting stillness.

Dino had looked around, too. I saw his shining blue eyes take in the gate, as if he planned a retreat if it should become necessary. I had an odd feeling that he would slide away like a fat, fuzzy spider and again disappear into some underground lair, and there were things I had to know and things I had to say. I blurted it all out quickly, "Dino, you're involved in something horrible. George Hobson sent me a letter. Then he was murdered. You've got to stop it—"

Bessie came waddling out the door, rapidly, a broom prudently in her hand, but her eyes rather wild. "Miz Lowry, it's the hurricane. It's that Edith. It's on the radio. All at once she's started across land, hard as she can go. Winds over a hundred miles an hour. We're right on the edge of it now." She paused. The bamboos crackled and murmured; the palm trees rattled, and Bessie said, "She's coming, that old Edith. Get in the house!" She turned to Dino. "And you get out. Go on!" She brandished her broom at Dino.

It was comic in a slapstick way and dreadful. Dino's glassy blue eyes slanted her way. Bessie waved the broom. I wanted Dino to leave; I knew now that I could scarcely bear ever to see him again. Yet I couldn't let him scuttle away and disappear again.

Dino, however, took the decision out of my hands. He said to Bessie, "I tell you I am Mrs. Lowry's husband. I stay here with her."

I said to Bessie, "It's all right." Then I saw the troubled look in Bessie's face and felt a queer, hot tremor of wind touch my face. "Bessie, do you want to go home?"

"It's my grandchildren, Miz Lowry. Two of them. In my house."

"You'll have to go then. Hurry, before the storm is worse."

Dino's eyes sparkled but he was uneasy too, listening and watching an odd swaying motion that started up among the bamboos and then checked itself. I was not afraid of Dino, I told myself again. So I made Bessie go home, which she did reluctantly, yet nervously listening as Dino was—and as I was, too. She went to the gate, where she paused to give me a troubled look. Then the gate slammed. Dino said, "This house looks strong."

"Dino, how did you find me? How did you know Dick is here? When—why did you come to Tampa?"

"I think we'd better go in the house."

But if it had been Blondie on the escalator, then of course she had had time while I shopped and drove around Tampa to tell Dino that she had seen me. How he found the house was a question I could not answer.

And then, unexpectedly, the tiny flicker of something like recognition came to life; it wasn't recognition in fact; it was a small but dreadful memory: a beatnik type—my British merchant friend had so described a man who had come to the door of George Hobson's curio shop, waited, looked "fishy" and then disappeared. Immediately George Hobson had got rid of me. So was George Hobson afraid of the beatnik type? Fat, my British friend had said, a beard. Fishy. And George Hobson had said in his letter, "I couldn't talk to you. Someone was listening." If it had been Dino, then he had seen me talking to George Hobson. I still didn't think Dino could have murdered George Hobson. But George Hobson had been murdered.

Dino said, "Don't stand there staring. Come on in the house."

The trees were rattling wildly; the glossy green leaves all around us seemed possessed of independent lives and were dancing and shaking. A branch of the enormous water oak

came crashing down into the patio. It was not large; it was
scarcely more than a sizable twig; the Spanish moss on it
looked gray like a spider web. Dino ran to the front of the
house. The wind made it hard for him to hold the door open.
I didn't want to enter that enclosed space with Dino; I
couldn't stay out in the patio. I followed him and he let me
pass him without touching me and I hurried into the wider
space of the living room. It was almost dark. I found a lamp
and turned it on. Dino took a breath and daintily smoothed
his disgusting long hair.

I turned on another lamp. Somehow it seemed to me that it
was necessary to have all the light I could. The living room
was all modern, pale woods and glass. The floor was terrazzo
here too, and there were enormous ottomans, brilliant red and
orange and green, white chairs and sofas, and white walls
and rugs. Ordinarily it must have been a bright and lively
room; then it only seemed lonely. Dino settled down on an
ottoman. I hadn't noticed until then that below that thick
light beard he wore a wide black tie, flowing a little as if he
were a Gay Nineties dandy, and a pink waistcoat. He looked
curiously effeminate with that long wavy hair, and curiously
evil.

There was a distinct thud and crash somewhere outside,
beyond the walls of the patio, I thought. Dino cocked his
head. "A tree?"

I said desperately, "Dino, you can't go on with this—"

"What are you talking about?"

"George Hobson's murder, of course. The letter he gave
me. The list of names and—"

I stopped, half frightened as Dino rose, sleekly as a very
fat cat. He looked very tall. His face was now in the shadow
of the lampshade. I could see his thick beard move. "Give me
this letter you say somebody sent you. This—whatever it is—
list of names of some kind."

Lying again, I thought, pretending he knows nothing about
any of it. But Dino started slowly toward me. I moved back.
There was suddenly a rush of air through the room, a door
crashed back, and someone seemed to catch it. Then I heard
Richard. "Marcia, it's a real hurricane!"

He came to the doorway, saw Dino and stopped. Dino had
whirled around. The two men eyed each other and there was
an enormous burst and surge of wind slapping at the shutters.

Dino advanced toward Richard. He held out his hand. He

said, unbelievably, "Well, my old friend. Quite a gathering. How have you been?"

Richard stood perfectly still. Dino's hand dropped back to his side. Finally Richard said, "So you've come back—"

Dino shoved his hands in his sagging pockets.

Richard came into the room. "Now we'll have a talk."

Dino's voice was silky and yet a little breathless. "Talk will get you nowhere. I'm staying here with my wife. A nice little *ménage à trois*. Delightful. How do we arrange things?"

Richard laughed. It was a perfectly honest, yet exasperated laugh, which infuriated Dino; his blue eyes took on that ugly glaze again. "Are you never going to grow up, Dino?" Richard said. "You're talking like a teen-ager trying to be sophisticated. What's that in your pocket?"

Dino backed away. Then I noticed that something heavy sagged down one pocket. "I'll show you whether I'm grown up," Dino said and pulled out a gun.

It was a rather small revolver but it was a revolver.

Richard said, "You're not going to use that, you know, Dino. But you'd better give it to me."

Dino turned the revolver in his hand. Suddenly he looked a little uneasy. "Well . . ." he said. "Well . . ."

"Come on. Give it to me." Richard went to Dino deliberately, grasped his wrist and took the gun. Dino didn't even struggle to keep it. "All right," he said sulkily. "You know I hate guns. I've always hated them."

The fact was that, secretly, Dino was afraid of guns. Richard said almost good-naturedly, "That's all right, Dino. I'll just unload this." He opened the gun and laughed again. "Not loaded. Why bother to carry it?"

He tossed the gun down on a chair. Dino looked a little sheepish. And all at once, from habit perhaps, a kind of cloak of civilization and ordinary behavior came upon us. Richard said, "I'll get something to drink."

Dino took a comb from some pocket, found a wall mirror and combed his long and wavy hair.

There was a clatter of ice from the kitchen. The wind pushed at the house and rattled the bolted shutters.

Dino said over his shoulder, watching his fat face in the mirror, "You're looking well, Marcia. Not much like that lumpy little kid I married because my father made me. Dear me"—he turned around, smiling—"the ugly duckling. You've turned into a really attractive woman. How glad I am that I've come back to you, my lovely wife."

Richard said from the doorway, "Bourbon or gin?" He put a tray down on a table.

"I'll help myself," Dino said and did so, all but filling the glass with gin. He added ice and about a drop of tonic. "I was only telling my wife how beautiful she has become and how glad I am to have returned to her."

Richard and I did not even look at each other. We both spoke. I said, "No. Our marriage is over, Dino."

Richard said, "Marcia is going to get a divorce."

Dino only smiled. "I knew something like that was in the wind. I suppose you want my agreement about this, don't you?"

"I wanted to tell you," I said.

Dino swaggered across to the fireplace and took up a proprietorlike position before the hearth. "You want to marry, you two. Probably high time. However, we'll let that go. I'm a man of the world. I'll not ask what's been going on while I was away. But divorce? Oh, no."

TEN

Again, oddly, something seemed to come down like a cloak of ordinary and conventional behavior, which in itself was strange, although I didn't think of it. I went to sit in a corner of a small sofa. Richard stood behind a chair, leaning his elbows on its back, watching Dino thoughtfully.

Perhaps because we had all been very young together and accustomed to one another, it seemed at once completely normal and utterly fantastic that we should be there, the three of us, talking with the candor that comes from old acquaintance.

Richard said, "Well, then. That is your decision. If you want to fight a divorce, you can. Marcia will charge desertion."

Dino caressed his bushy beard. "But I was kidnapped. That's not desertion."

"You can prove, then, that you were kidnapped?" Richard's voice was perfectly calm.

"You're talking like a lawyer."

"I am a lawyer. Marcia could have had a divorce from you by now on the charge of desertion—"

"But she wouldn't," Dino said, stroking his beard. "And even if she had claimed that I deserted her and then later I turned up, having been held against my will, kidnapped, all that—her divorce and a marriage between you two, which the divorce would have made possible, would certainly have put you both in a questionable situation." Dino was very smug. "I can see that difficulties might have arisen. Especially if I had chosen to protest the divorce and marriage."

"It might have been a bore," Richard said. "But since you are alive and—"

Dino cut in again. "Were you very disappointed to find me in your little hideaway neither dead nor kidnapped?"

"Frankly I'd prefer never to have any news of you at all," Richard said coolly. "Marcia felt differently."

"Naturally. She wants me back."

"No. You're quite mistaken about that. Marcia is through with you, Dino, like it or lump it."

"Then why did she go all the way to Hong Kong to try to find me? She said she'd been there. Doesn't look much like she's through with me, does it?"

Richard sat down, looked thoughtfully at Dino and after a moment said seriously, "I honestly don't think you would understand why she tried to find you."

Dino laughed. "Plain as the nose on your face. She's still in love with me. Wouldn't marry you until she'd given me another—another chance."

"No, that's not the reason," Richard said, still very calmly and seriously. "It was because she was once married to you—"

"She's still married to me."

Richard said nothing for a moment. His quiet eyes seemed to measure and plumb for depths in Dino which were not there. He said at last, "There's no use in trying to explain."

Dino laughed again. Then he shambled across the room, his long hair swinging. He refilled his glass, adding again a bare splash of tonic, and I thought, parenthetically, that Dino should not drink so much.

The wind gave a shriek outside and then lowered to a rush and rattle again. Dino came back and took up his position before the fireplace. "I'll tell you what I understand," he said, grinning behind the fuzzy beard. "Marica feels that she's still my wife. So she wouldn't marry you, Dick. Obvious. You try to imply reasons which are so high and noble that they are beyond my understanding. You're after my wife, maybe you've had her—"

Richard's voice was like a whiplash. "All right, Dino, that's enough of that."

Dino backed away as if Richard had started toward him. "Now, wait a minute, wait a minute. I didn't say anything, I mean—well, all I have to say is I'm not going to consent to this fine friendly divorce you want. Clear?"

"It really doesn't matter, you know." Richard held hard to the chair as if he had to control his fists. "She has grounds for a divorce. But there's a second thing you must understand. We haven't told the police anything about the murder of George Hobson—"

Dino's voice lifted to a squeal. "Murder—why, why—I know nothing of any murder! Marcia keeps talking about some guy by the name of Hobson and a letter and some sort of list. What's it all about?"

But he knew. I was sure of it. Richard glanced at me and I nodded. "I told him George Hobson had sent me the letter and the list. He denies knowing George Hobson. But I think Dino was the man in the doorway of the curio shop. A beatnik type, the Englishman said. Look at him."

"So you heard Marcia ask George Hobson about that piece of jade, did you, Dino?" Richard said.

Dino squealed again, "I tell you I don't know what you're talking about!"

Richard waited a moment, thoughtfully. Then he said, as if idly curious, "You say *you* found *us*, Dino. How did that happen?"

"Followed you from—" Dino began to speak boastfully, but his eyes shot to me and I knew that he had been caught in the web of one of his own lies. He scuttled back to the lie. "Why, really, it was the oddest thing. You might say it was fate. I actually saw Marcia on the street. Simply followed her here. Easy as that. Fate. Or my good luck—"

Richard's face did not change and he couldn't have said more clearly that he didn't believe Dino.

Dino floundered more deeply into his foolish little web. "Fate. I had—had taken passage on a ship to Tampa. Cargo ship. From Bangkok, you know. Arrived, started out to find a hotel and to phone home, get in touch with Marcia, of course. Tell her I had escaped my kidnappers. I meant to phone her, phone my father . . ." He laughed a little. "Prodigal's return, you know. Fatted calf. Well, I didn't hope for that really, still —and there was Marcia herself. Felt as if I was dreaming actually, in broad daylight. Right there on the street. So she took a taxi and I got another one and followed her—"

I wanted to say, You didn't follow me. You were here when I came back—but Richard stopped me. "Don't strain your imagination too much. You didn't come by ship. You came by plane. You followed us from—probably from Hong Kong. You followed us because we stopped in San Francisco and I saw John Smith."

Dino suddenly and smugly smiled behind that fuzzy beard. He could not resist a boastful admission "You didn't get anything out of him!" He didn't seem to know that he had, in a few words, refuted his own lies . . . that, or he didn't care.

The wind suddenly charged upon the house as if we three, the glass table before us, the house itself were its sole targets for destruction. Dino backed away from the fireplace as if the chimney might hold some danger. He said, "I hope this house is safe. Seemed to be well built; I took a look when I came into the patio—"

I said, "Dick, I think Blondie is here, too. I think I saw her."

"Here?"

"In Tampa, yes. In a store. I'm not sure, though."

There was the faintest little smirk within Dino's beard. Richard said, "So you and the woman came together. All right! We'll turn over Hobson's note and the list he gave us to the Hong Kong police. In the meantime," Richard said very deliberately, "you can get out before I kick you out."

"Oh, now, don't be hasty, Dick." Dino looked really concerned. He slid over to a window and fumbled at the curtains, which Bessie had drawn across it. The heavy red silk drapery parted but showed only dark glass, for Bessie had also closed and fastened the shutters. I saw a dim reflection of the room, Richard standing, very tall and still, a glitter from light wood and glass, and Dino's fattish face and long hair.

"You can't send me out into a storm like this." Dino let the curtain fall and turned. He looked at me for a moment and then, holding his glass in one hand, came over to me. He put his other hand under my chin and I forced myself not to move. His hand felt moist and ugly. His eyes were oddly veiled and his face flushed. "Darling," he said, laughed and turned to Richard, "I left a dull little schoolgirl for a wife. I come back to find a beauty. Well, here I am and here I stay. With my wife."

Richard said, "You'll have to stay, I suppose, till the storm is over. Not with Marcia."

"But she's my wife," Dino insisted. His speech was becoming slurred. He waved his glass, which was now empty again and said, "Just give me a drink, Dick, old fellow. I'm the prodigal son returned, remembered. Fatted calf. Wonder if he had a wife."

"You're drunk," Richard said. "You'd better get some food in you."

Dino considered it, still holding my chin. "I've changed my mind. Tell you what I'll do," he said unexpectedly. "I'll make a bargain with you. I'll come clean. I do want that letter. I want that list too. Then—then promise to forget the whole thing." He began to grin with a foolish attempt at camaraderie. "I know you, Dick. You'd never go back on your word, old fellow. So give me your word that you'll forget the letter, forget the whole thing. And you can have my wife. I don't want her, anyway. Never did. That was my father's doing, our marriage. Told me he'd never give me another cent unless I married her. Forget the whole thing. Fair—fair trade," Dino mumbled and then added a comic frightening touch to the scene. His moist hand dropped away from my chin, he gave me a glassy stare, and quite slowly knelt down, crumpled and sagged over on the floor.

"Dick, he's had a—a heart attack!"

"He's had too much to drink too fast."

We both stared down at Dino's slack figure. His nose and part of his beard were buried in the rug. Richard came and turned him over. Dino's mouth fell open and he gave a loud, raucous and perfectly preposterous snore. It was dreadful and again comic. I remember that I thought briefly how right I had been to show no fear of Dino. Nobody could be afraid of that limp and ridiculous figure on the rug.

Richard glanced at the sofa which was small, modern and so austere that I could not imagine anyone taking comfort from it. There was a scattering of bright red and green cushions on its adamant surface, so Richard took one, brought it back and shoved it not too gently under Dino's lolling head.

We then simply looked at him again for a moment. Richard said finally, "We'll have to keep him here till he gets himself together. Marcia, what *do* you think he's up to?"

I rose.

"I don't know. But something—something he's afraid to talk about. Something that scares him. But something he's determined to go on with."

"Did you tell him what Hobson wrote in the letter?"

"No. No, I only said he had sent me the letter and—I think I told Dino that he couldn't go on with it."

"You didn't say that Hobson never told you exactly what he meant by 'dangerous'?"

"No, that's all I told him."

"Then of curse he thinks we know more than we actually do," Richard said slowly. "I'm not sure that's a good idea. Somebody wasn't afraid to kill Hobson. The letter wasn't as explicit as Dino seems to think it is. Maybe it would be better —safer, anyway—to tell Dino that Hobson didn't name names."

"But he did name names. That is, the list—"

"Not real names. But if we turn over the list to the police they may be able to trace the real names. I don't know what is best to do." Suddenly Richard said, "Why, of course! I know how he found this place! If you really saw Blondie, she may have told him she had seen you. But it was Gil Rayburn. I mean, that's how Dino guessed where to find you! He knows Gil. That is, he really doesn't know him, but Gil was in New York a few times and I remember that they met. Dino remembered him, all right, and his name, and simply went to the Tampa phone book. He didn't come by ship. He followed us—I think from Hong Kong. From San Francisco. He guessed we would try the Tampa name. Are you sure you saw Blondie here?"

"It was on the escalator in a store; we passed each other. I'm not sure it was Blondie. Different wig but same—same something. I thought, That's Blondie."

"Same way of moving? Same posture? Oh, there are a hundred ways of recognition. Dark glasses, I suppose."

"Oh, yes. I tried to get a better look at her but she'd gone. There were crowds of people shopping. I couldn't have found her."

"She could have followed us from San Francisco. I suppose she could have followed you here from the store."

"I told the taxi driver to take me to the pier. Tampa *is* a port, a big one. And then the driver made a kind of quick sight-seeing trip around the city. If Blondie followed me I didn't know it. And if she did—no, she couldn't have told Dino about this house because he was here when I came home. There wasn't time. He must have remembered your friend Gil and taken the chance, and Bessie said he forced his way in and—" I glanced down at Dino. "What are we going to do?"

Dino snored. The wind roared at the house. Richard said slowly, "I still can't see Dino killing anybody. Same reason I can't see him involved in any kind of espionage. He's—I don't know, he's just not the type to kill anybody."

"No. No, he isn't." Yet I must have doubted, somewhere in my instinct, for the words came out too strongly. I repeated it, though, "He couldn't have done that. He couldn't have taken a knife and—"

"Cut Hobson's throat? He did have a gun when he came here but it was like taking candy from a baby to take it away from him. Easier," Richard said, wincing. "I once tried to take candy from my sister's baby. He was cutting teeth at the time."

"The gun wasn't loaded. But you know Dino; he simply hasn't much sense of right or wrong. He was born that way."

"You've felt sorry for him too many times," Richard said shortly. "And if you'll ever forgive me for saying so, as you probably won't, his father has worked on your kindness and your loyalty too many times."

"What about you, Richard?" I said softly.

He looked a little taken aback but said vigorously, "No, I'm not sorry for Dino!"

Dino's jacket had fallen apart, showing the ludicrous pink velvet waistcoat. I could also see the very edge of a wallet in his pocket. I said, "Look in his pockets."

"Good heavens!" Richard knelt down. He took out a wallet first, took one look inside it, sat back on his heels and said, "Good Lord!"

I knelt down too and looked and really couldn't have said anything. The wallet was stuffed with bills.

"Hundred-dollar bills," Richard said in an awed way.

The wind shrieked and seemed to blow through the house almost as if a door had opened somewhere. I remember that the rug below my hand quivered as the wind moved it. "How many?"

"I don't know. It must run to thousands of dollars. Where did he get all this?"

The wind had not flung open a door. A man behind us said, "All right, stand up. No tricks. Drop that wallet."

I scrabbled around on the rug, still on my knees. Richard rose slowly. The man standing in the doorway wore a hat, pulled low, dripping with rain; he wore a dripping, glittering, raincoat. He had a revolver in his hand and looked as if he intended to use it. We stayed like that, none of us moving, until Dino gave another rasping snore and the man with the revolver said, "Give me that wallet. Toss it to me." He took an unnervingly steady and concentrated aim with his revolver so that its little black eye pointed straight at me. Richard said, "Foolish. I could identify you, you know, if you shot her."

"You wouldn't be in a position to identify anybody. The wallet—"

"All right," Richard said, tossed it at the man's head and jumped for him. He ducked and pulled the trigger of the revolver. The roar and crash and smell filled the room, and the wind roared, too, and Dino gave another snort and pulled himself up on his elbow. The man in the raincoat recovered his balance and aimed at me again. Dino rubbed his face and his beard and mumbled something that made no sense. The man in the doorway said sharply, "*You!* Get on your feet."

Dino got up, holding on to a chair. He stood and swayed and rubbed his puffy face. He then seemed to take in something of what was going on and shambled out past the man, who kept his revolver aimed at me. Richard said, "Don't move, Marcia," quite calmly really and also unnecessarily. I couldn't have moved.

Dino disappeared. The man in the doorway snatched up the wallet, keeping a very steady eye on Richard and a steady grip on his revolver. Then he too disappeared and the wind howled through the house, curling up the rug and waving the curtains.

Richard ran into the hall.

There wasn't a chance of pursuing the two men. When Richard came back, his coat was wet, and his dark hair plastered down with wind and rain. "He had a taxi waiting. He dragged Dino into the cab and the lights shot off down the street." Richard took off his dripping coat, shook it and said, "I hadn't bolted the gate. Hadn't even locked the door. I didn't expect Dino. Or the man we may as well call Jones, and that is certainly not his name."

ELEVEN

It was surmise, but it seemed a likely surmise that it was Jones: he had known Dino; he followed him to the house. So he and probably Blondie had known exactly where Dino went. "He, or they," Richard said, "must have grown impatient. Either that, or both of them know Dino's weak head for drinking and were afraid he'd say too much. They want that Hobson letter. They're afraid the list might put the police on their track. It doesn't really matter how Dino and, if you are right, Blondie managed to get here. The man listed as Herbert Jones is certainly their ally. It could only have been the fake Jones."

"He must have paid the taxi driver a fortune to get him to come out here, with trees going down in the storm."

"They seem to have money to pay, all right. Whatever they're doing must be profitable. They're sure that the Hobson letter and the list can stop their operation."

I had behaved, it seems to me, quite admirably up to then. But now I screamed and pointed. Incredulous, Richard stared down unbelievingly at some small scarlet drops on the white rug. "Well, by golly, I didn't even know he hit me."

"Let me see—"

"I'm bleeding all over the rug."

"*Let me see!*" He gave me his knife so I could slit up his sleeve, and as Richard said, it was only a scratch. But to me it looked like something terrifying—it reminded me of the redness around little George Hobson's thin throat.

However, Richard said that he could not stand there and drip gore on his host's rug. We got into the nearest bathroom and he took off his shirt. We washed the wound with soap and water and found an antiseptic which, when liberally applied by me, brought forth such a howl on Richard's part that I felt it must be efficacious. We found gauze and adhesive and made quite a neat bandage, but it was some time before we could stop the bleeding. I had used up several bandages, shuddering as I dropped the red, sodden little pieces in the wastebasket, before eventually the bleeding subsided to a

kind of slow ooze and Richard said that he thought now that
he'd live and it wouldn't hurt me to have a drink. It wouldn't
hurt him, either, he said, and led the way back to the living
room. The drops of red looked dreadful on the rug, so I got
cold water and towels and began to work on them before
they had time to set.

"Carnage, no less," Richard said. "Here, I'll help."

We weren't very satisfied with the patchy wet results of
our labors, and the wind roared and a tree went down somewhere quite close and shook the house. We gathered up all
the towels and paper tissues and took them to the kitchen incinerator.

Richard looked around. "That Bessie is a jewel. She's left
us food!" We moved all the covered, enticing plates into the
Spanish dining room and ravenously ate ham and salad and
some kind of pie, and listened to the wind and the torrents of
rain pounding the house, the patio, the whole world; it
seemed to me as if it would never cease.

Once Richard looked down at his bare chest and the bandage on his arm and said with mild surprise, "A gent should
wear a coat at dinner." He went off toward his room and
came back with a blue pajama jacket across his shoulders.
"Elegant dinner attire!"

He looked at me and said, "Well, Dino's gone again. He's
got to be in Tampa for the night at least. We can't get to the
police tonight. They'll have their hands full anyway in this
storm. But tomorrow morning we can, Marcia. I know how
you feel. But the police are the instruments of law and
order—"

"*No!*" I had learned some things about Richard; one was
that he was willing to listen to another person's viewpoint; he
might not accept it, but he listened. I went on quickly, "Dino
didn't do anything illegal here in Tampa. We don't believe
that he killed George Hobson. We only think that he knows
something about it."

"We *know*. He admitted his knowledge when he asked us
to give him the letter. He also admitted knowing about the
San Francisco man."

"Yes, but that doesn't mean he murdered Hobson. Dick,
consider—what evidence of anything illegal could we tell the
police here?"

Richard frowned a little but answered honestly, "All right,
not much factual evidence. But the Hobson letter is evidence—"

"—for Inspector Filladon in Hong Kong."

"That doesn't matter. The police here could communicate with him. We believe that you have been followed. We believe a woman tried to get the letter and the list, and we believe that she is in Tampa. We know that a man came with a gun and got Dino away. We know that Dino's wallet was stuffed with hundred-dollar bills, and people like Dino don't carry that much cash around, not for any legitimate purpose."

He stopped right there, as if struck by an ugly notion.

I didn't arrive at the same notion then but it was perhaps knocking at the door of my awareness, for I busied myself very energetically clearing the table and bustling around the kitchen and carrying coffee into the bright and pleasant living room. Apart from the raging storm outside, it was very silent. Richard was deep in obviously troubled thought. After a while a series of little thuds came from somewhere in the house and I set down my coffee cup with a crash. Richard looked up. "Sounds like a loose shutter somewhere. I'll fix it."

I stopped him. "You can't do anything with that arm!"

He moved it tentatively and then more briskly. "I can pound in a nail."

"You'll start it bleeding again."

"Honestly, Marcia, it really is only a nick; I'm not a stretcher case."

"I don't want you to become one!" I said shortly and went back to our argument. "If we tell the police the little we know, what could they do here—what would they have reason to do? Hunt for a man who might have a gun? Hunt for Dino because we want him found? All they could possibly say is that—well, I suppose, that they would look into it."

"All right. We'll wait. I promised you to do what you want done if I can. There may come a time when I can't keep that promise."

"Dick, I know that I'm wrong in a way. But if the thing, whatever it is, can be stopped, straightened out, something done—"

His face was rather white and very troubled. "George Hobson was stopped."

"Were you right about the other post-office box too?"

"I don't know. I found a box with the right number. It was in the main post office, same as in San Francisco. But after these two days of waiting for him I decided that I was watching at the wrong hours—if, that is, he makes regular visits. The post office is open all night—not the windows, but the main door—so anybody can get to the boxes. I decided to come back here and try again tonight. Then I realized that it was a real storm and dashed in without bolting the gate behind me. Herbert Jones wanted to get Dino out of the house. He didn't tell us to hand over the letter. Maybe Dino hasn't let him know about it yet. If he hasn't, he soon will, though. As I remember him, Dino sobers up as fast as he passes out. By now I would think that Jones knows all about the list and the letter. They've had to work fast, Dino and Blondie. Now the code will have to be changed. The fake names, everything. It wouldn't surprise me," Richard said glumly, "if the whole list, the whole club converges here."

The list of anonymous names, the conspiracy—whatever it was, "the club" was as good a name as any for it. The loose shutter banged and both of us jumped as if somebody were trying to force his way into the house. Richard said, "I'll see about that shutter. I really wouldn't care to have Mr. Jones crawling into the house. Or Dino either, drunk or sober."

It was a chilling thought. I went with him and we explored the house; it was small as to the number of rooms but they were large rooms. The shutter was hanging by a broken hinge outside the window of an enormous bedroom, on the corner beyond my room. Bessie had apparently forgotten to latch that window. Richard pushed it up, leaned out to examine the hinge and said that there would probably be a hammer and nails somewhere. So we explored again and found a small kind of furnance- and tool-room and laundry at the other end of the house.

Back in the bedroom Richard crawled out into the darkness and rain and pounded away at the shutter, nailing it firmly in place. Rain gushed in. Richard was crawling back into the room when the lights went out. When he banged down the window, one of his fingers got caught and he told me to get candles from the dining room table. I groped my way through the hall, into the dining room, struck my elbow on a chair and found a silver candelabrum on the table, matches beside it. The room, the house wavered into light as I touched matches to the candles and I went back to the bedroom, where Richard was sucking his finger and quietly swearing. When the window was properly bolted we went back to the living room, which looked different in the candlelight, not so bright and pleasant but rather queerly cold. Richard's blue pajama jacket was drenched and the rain had soaked through the bandage on his arm so the vicious little wound, which he called a nick, had started to bleed slowly. We put more antiseptic on it and a fresh bandage. Then Richard took a candle, went back to his host's bedroom and returned with a stack of wildly colored sport shirts. "Gil is about my size," he explained and draped the wet pajama jacket over a chair. He put on one of the shirts which, in the flickering candlelight, did look rather peculiar, as if its colors danced together. "Gil must have been to Hawaii," he said, eying the shirt.

Presently he went to a small chest of drawers and unearthed a transistor radio. We listened, absently, until at last the announcer told us that, incredibly, Edith was moving out over the Gulf and that we were very lucky to have escaped the hurricane. The wind shrieked and the radio stopped in the middle of a word of revolting cheer. "Station was knocked off the air," Richard said. "Serves him right."

The wind howled, the rain drove down on the house, and we went to bed early. Richard took one candle again, left the candelabrum for me on the night table, said briefly that I'd better not open the French doors leading to the patio (as if I would), and walked firmly away, which didn't exactly boost my spirits. Chivalry and tact are no doubt admirable qualities, but not in the middle of a howling hurricane, in a house where a gun had been fired and there was blood on the rug. And Dino had been there. Dino.

The house was still charming, yet that night it seemed different. Dino had been there, yes. But his living presence also seemed to have left something behind—something intangible but alive, too, and threatening, for an ugly spectre, a nightmarish fantasy crept out of the wavering shadows. I was sure that it was the dreadful notion which had turned Richard so white and sober. I could see why he said that there might come a time when he could no longer keep his promise to me to protect Dino. I wouldn't accept my hideous notion as an explanation of anything. I wouldn't even put it into words. I wouldn't speak of it to Richard for fear I would only reinforce his own fear. I wouldn't—unless I had to.

But in enlisting Richard's help, against his judgment, I had taken on a heavy responsibility. He promised to help because he loved me. It seemed likely that he also still had a kind of feeling of old-time—not friendliness, but certainly something like good will for Dino in spite of everything.

Yet if my notion proved to be true, the business of fake names and post-office-box numbers was more than thoroughly explained. When people engage in an illegal activity and have need to communicate with each other, it is obviously safer for them to use names that don't belong to them and no real addresses. But then, we had known that from the time we had seen the remarkably anonymous list of names and scrambled letters and numbers. People who engage in legitimate affairs do not try to hide their names.

Once the police had a full report of Hobson's letter, the Hobson murder and the list, I had no doubt they would be able to trace the men behind the names. The list was thus almost as dangerous to them as the Hobson letter. The police could find Dino. Mr. Lowry had begged me to give Dino another chance. I wondered if perhaps Mr. Lowry had secretly meant not only "give Dino another chance at marriage" but "if Dino is involved in something shady, give him another chance about that, help him."

I could not guess at Mr. Lowry's thoughts.

And just then there was nothing I could do. I went to sleep at last, telling myself that people could carry large sums of money around for perfectly legitimate reasons.

I had left one candle burning. When I awoke I smelled burnt wick and wax. I knew then that somebody was in the room. The wind was still shrieking, the rain was still pounding, yet in the room itself there had been some movement, something stealthy and so terrifying that I couldn't move, so naturally, quickly, before I let myself stop and think about it, I did move. I rolled over the far edge of the bed, over to the thick rug, let myself down and rolled under the bed, very, very swiftly. An animal could not have done it better. There was a dust flounce of chintz and I pushed under it. My face pressed into the thick rug. After an agonizingly long moment a light showed dimly, shooting here and there, and I knew it was a flashlight.

Below the chintz flounce I thought I could see movement, then the darting light went out. I also thought that I could hear a kind of scuttling movement, like a crab in the sand. Abruptly wind and rain burst into the room from the patio. Another kind of light came, a wavering, flickering light. Richard said from the door, "What's the matter? Where are—" He stopped.

"I'm under the bed," I shouted above the wind.

He must have gone to close the door to the patio. I heard it bang hard and the wind in the room lessened. I crawled out from under the bed and sneezed.

Richard was standing next to the bed. He didn't so much as look at me; he was looking down.

I saw it then, a long knife. It was a kitchen knife, a carving knife, viciously sharp. It lay on the table beside the bed.

TWELVE

I said, "It's a knife." It was not a great contribution. I could only remember little George Hobson as I had seen him behind his counter. Richard said, "Did you see who was here?"

"How could I? It was dark."

"There was a light, looked like a flashlight." He gave me a look then. "You'd better sit down. Get something around you. You'll catch your death," he said, infringing upon Mrs. Clurg's copyright and favorite advice.

I had been spry enough rolling under the bed. Now I couldn't possibly move and my teeth were chattering in a perfectly idiotic way. Richard saw my white dressing gown crumpled on the chaise longue and put it around my shoulders. "Searched, didn't he?"

He—whoever he was—had searched. Closet, drawers and my suitcase, and my handbag, which had been opened and everything in it spilled out on the floor. The zipper part of it gaped open. Lipstick, tiny comb, compact, coin purse, everything was on the floor, including my wallet and my traveler's checks.

Richard picked up my handbag. "A good thing the letter and the list were not here. Hobson must have made whoever murdered him believe that his letter was very specific."

"That . . . that knife." I picked it up unsteadily, thinking of George Hobson.

"Yes." Richard's face was white in the flickering candlelight and hard as a rock. But he said, trying to ease my shock, "Whoever it was probably only wanted to be sure he could cut his way into your suitcase or—or something. Don't look like that." He put his arms close around me and I leaned against him. My teeth still chattered, but I told myself to believe him and I felt better for a moment.

Then he said soberly, "They think we know more than we know. They realize that you and I are dangerous to them."

Hobson had said "Very dangerous."

"Dick, did he—did whoever was here—did he intend to murder *me?*"

85

"Nonsense! I told you. Wanted the knife to cut open your suitcase if he had to, or pry open the door or . . . I'm going to get some coffee. Come on—"

I wanted to believe him. I didn't. He made sure the patio door was bolted, as it had been, securely, until whoever crept into the house had flung the door open to make his escape.

We went to the kitchen, forgetting that there was no electricity so we couldn't make coffee. We settled for a whiskey and soda, since attempted murder (And murder of me! I thought with utter disbelief) was certainly an excuse for nighttime drinking. There were cushions on the living-room floor; Richard had been trying to sleep there and keep an eye on the house, but said wryly that he had shut the eye.

I had done him an injustice. I swallowed more whiskey.

"I thought I'd know it if somebody really did get in the house. I must have gone to sleep. I woke up and thought I saw a kind of glancing light from the hall that leads to your room, so I came and whoever was there must have heard me, unbolted the patio door and got away."

I was feeling a little more like myself, not much but a little. "How did he get in the house?"

"I've a nasty feeling that he was *in* the house. Somewhere. Came in through that loose shutter before I fixed it. He was probably hiding in the bathroom or a clothes closet in Gil's bedroom while I nailed the shutter. But I searched the house after you went to bed. I don't think I missed any place big enough to hide a cat." He stared at me for a second, said, "Yes, I did," and took the candle with him out of the room. I sat in the darkness and would have gibbered to myself if it hadn't been for the whiskey. So I swigged away until the candle and Richard came back. He said with quite fearful self-disgust, "Sure. I missed it. The furnace."

I had swigged a little too heartily. I said "Furnace?" and giggled.

He didn't slap me but looked as if he'd like to, and that was not at all the way a hero who has just saved his girl from a fate worse than death ought to look. Except it wasn't a fate worse than death, I thought muzzily. It was—well, it was very likely intended to be murder itself. Richard took the glass from me. But the whiskey was all gone, so I giggled again and he said, "If you have hysterics now I promise to shake the very hell out of you."

A moment of sweet reason whisked over me. "How could anybody hide in a furnace?"

"Somebody could in this one. As long as it wasn't turned on, and of course it wasn't. It's like a big box with a heating unit in the middle of it. He wouldn't even have to be acquainted with the house."

"It couldn't have been Dino! He's too big, for one thing."

"Whoever was there—if he was, and I can't think of any other place I didn't search—wouldn't have had to stay there long. Remember, the lights had gone out. We sat listening to the radio."

It was not nice to think that someone had been in the house, waiting. The kitchen knife proved to be one of a set. The rest of the set was in a kitchen drawer. That was not nice, either.

We spent what was left of the night in Richard's room. I curled up under a blanket on his bed and he prowled the house at intervals and returned to smoke and think. We didn't talk much. For one thing, the violence of the storm had a queerly hypnotic effect; I had to listen to it. But for another thing, I didn't know what Richard intended to do and I didn't want to ask him. Once, though, he disappeared for quite a while and when he came back he had a revolver in his hand. "Gil's," he said briefly. "Found the shells for it too." He loaded it methodically. After that the revolver was never far from Richard's hand.

As the gray light of dawn straggled through the shutters Richard made a decision. "The situation has changed," he said. "I've got to talk to Dino. I've got to get hold of him somehow. He wants the letter. Probably all the men, the whole list—the whole club—want the letter. But somebody will come here. Our visitor last night believed that you must have the letter. There wasn't time to search my room and chances are they'll decide that I have the letter. You'll go home, Marcia, as soon as we can get a taxi."

"No."

"Yes."

He went to the telephone. But he couldn't call a taxi, he couldn't call the police even if he had intended to, he couldn't phone anybody, for the telephone wasn't working. There wasn't even a dial tone. "I suppose the storm knocked it out," he said, coming back. "I don't want you here, Marcia. It's too much like staking out bait for a tiger. But I've got to get Dino here, try to make him talk because—" He stopped abruptly.

I said, almost in a whisper, "Yes. I thought of that, too."

He gave me a quick look, and then paced the floor back and forth several times before he replied. When he came to a stop, his face was strained and white again. "It's the money Dino had. The cash. Straightforward business is simply not transacted with cash. People want check records. Nobody likes to carry around so much cash. There's no real need to carry it for any legal undertakings."

"No."

"Of course it's been on your mind, too."

"I couldn't help it. Dino's been in the East so long. We don't know what he was doing. He was in Far Eastern countries where it's said to be easier to get. Those names . . . men living in port cities."

"If it's dope smuggling—'evil' is a strong word. But if that's it, we are evil too if we try to protect Dino."

"You needn't stick to your promise to me, Dick. If you really think that's it—but it would kill Mr. Lowry."

"Better that, perhaps, than take part ourselves in the slow murder of God knows how many people."

"I'll do whatever you say."

"If it's dope smuggling it's too big for me. But it's fair to make sure. I'll stay here. Dino, or one of them, will come back. I'll do what I can do. But you're to go home."

I said "All right," merely to satisfy him. I had no intention of going home just then.

THIRTEEN

Once the words were out—dope smuggling and the possibility of Dino's taking part in it—a curious uncertainty came over me. Put into words, the hypothesis didn't seem quite so likely. In a way I think Richard felt the same way, for once he said that he really didn't think Dino would be such a fool. "He's intelligent enough. He knows that he'd be sticking his neck out. Yet he's been in the Far East for a long time. Opium, say, or heroin. Small amounts smuggled into the country could bring in quite a sizable amount of money to the men of the—the club. The list of names, distributors perhaps. He arranged, or somebody arranged, a deal with the men on the list, all of them living in port cities. It may have been a coincidence, but it suggests smuggling. It is obviously something so secret and dangerous to them that they settled on this business of fake names and post-office-box numbers. Obviously they had to have a way to communicate with each other. It looks as if, also, they had to have some way of sending, say packages to each other, or money. I think that they decided on this in the hope it would give them some slight self-protection. But they know that once the authorities get so much as a whiff of the list, coupled with the Hobson letter, they don't have a hope of escape. George Hobson had the list of fake names. So it looks as if he was to have something to do with whatever it is they are engaged in. But he didn't like it. He gave Mr. Lowry a hint. He must have been afraid to come out with the facts, yet he was decent enough to warn you. And whatever it is, somebody killed him. Somebody came here last night to find that letter." He said again gravely, "Whoever they are, Dino and Company, they believe that the letter is specific, clear, and dangerous to them."

He paced up and down. I went to open the curtains but then didn't want to open the windows. By this time streaks of sunlight sifted in through the shutters. Richard went on, "So Dino—the club—believes that we know more than in fact we do. The letter is evidence in its way but it is very incomplete evidence. They don't know that. So you see . . ." He came back to me. "I said that leaving you here in this house was like staking out bait for a tiger—"

"They know that you know too. You will be bait too."

"That's different."

"Even you can be illogical." I was tired and getting snappish and also frightened. So I said firmly and obstinately, "If you make me go home now, I'll go straight to the police and tell them we think Dino Lowry is smuggling dope."

"Oh, no, you won't. And, honestly, it's hard for me to believe that Dino would enter such a dangerous kind of thing as dope smuggling. There are all kinds of ramifications, underworld tentacles. We actually have no real evidence. All the same, I've got to get hold of Dino again, somehow, and make him talk. I've got to make sure that it isn't that. He'll come back here."

"Are you sure of that?"

"No," he said flatly.

So we stayed.

Neither of us wanted to stay but neither of us could accept the alternatives, one of which would be to take the whole story, such as it was, to the police there in Tampa, and we had no real evidence of anything. Another alternative was to go home, and leave Dino and the men on the list free to go on with whatever they were doing and forget the whole thing as Dino had proposed—and if the thing did prove to be dope smuggling then we were almost as guilty as they. A third alternative was to take the entire problem back to Inspector Filladon; we didn't even talk of that. And certainly, at that point we couldn't have called a taxi, and walking would have invited attack.

Strangely, too, yet naturally, we both felt something like responsibility for Dino. After all, Richard had known him most of his life, and he had been my husband. He still was my husband, I reminded myself, but that seemed entirely unreal. Now he didn't even look like the Dino I had married.

If Dino did come back to the house, there might be something we could do. We both felt, then, that if he didn't come back to the house we would not be able to find him.

I began to think of the man who had crept into my room carrying that ugly kitchen knife and who had escaped with swift cunning, as the tiger. If the tiger came back to the baited trap we might be able to get him, whoever and whatever he was, but it was very uncertain.

There were moments when each of us felt sure that we were wrong to stay in that house, to try to make it a trap. Sometimes the moments coincided, but we stayed.

The first day was calm and bright. In spite of our nightmarish reasons for being in the house at all, a kind of matter-of-fact domesticity settled upon us. The sheer physical labor of cleaning up the patio after the storm was a boon to both of us.

The devastation caused by the storm was appalling. The old water oak still stood as it had probably stood through many winds but the tiny white orchids were gone, only their roots clinging to the old oak. Long, ghostly wisps of Spanish moss cluttered the paths and shrubbery. The bamboos alone seemed intact, as if storms were their natural element. Gardenias lay here and there in dreary, muddy little humps, already yellow. The whole patio looked as if it had been under shellfire, it was so strewn with branches and foliage—all the claptrap a hurricane leaves behind it. We found a child's roller skate, which seemed remarkable, and a man's silk hat, which seemed really mysterious. Richard held it up; it was muddy and battered but it *was* a silk hat. "I haven't seen one of these in actual use since I was a child." He started to stick it on his head but stopped when he saw and smelled the mud it had contrived to collect. We worked with our hands; we worked with a shovel and a rake Richard found in a little toolhouse behind the bamboos. I put a fresh bandage on Richard's arm. The wound was obviously healing, although I could tell, as he worked, that his arm was stiff and painful.

The electricity had come on again quite early and the little fountain in the pool was bubbling. Bessie did not come.

Neither did Dino. Neither did Blondie, nor Herbert Jones, but we weren't expecting any of them, not in the full light of day. The stifling heaviness of the previous day was gone and the sky was a clear and incredibly innocent blue, as if it had never heard of such a thing as a hurricane, let alone engaged in one.

Evening came and still no Bessie, and still the telephone did not give a dial tone. Richard tried it over and over again, soberly. But it was nearly dark when we had our first indication that the tiger was showing an interest in the trap—far too much interest, as a matter of fact.

We were sitting on the patio having coffee when Richard rose, saying, "Let's just see if anything happens." He went to the gate, pulled the bolt and opened it; almost instantly he slammed it shut again and something spat sharply into it.

I ran to him. "*What—*"

"Somebody with a gun, hiding in that clump of palmettoes across the street."

"Dino?"

"It's too dark to see. But—no, Dino really is afraid of guns. I don't think it was Dino."

"Then . . . the man last night who came and took Dino away? The man we think got into the house? Jones?"

"Maybe." He gave me a troubled look. "Our little trap could be a trap for us. That's a cheerful thought."

It was by no means a cheerful thought. Richard sat down and sipped some coffee. "I suppose they've cut the telephone wires," he said. "By now the city should have all the phones in order—I mean those that the storm brought down."

"I can't imagine Dino cutting a telephone wire. He wouldn't know how!"

"It can't be difficult. I only hope the whole club hasn't gathered here to rally around Dino. I really don't want to take on the whole batch of them. I should have made you get out of here some way and go home, kicking and screaming if necessary."

And I would have kicked and screamed, too, I thought but was frightened.

Richard sighed. "We'll have to play it by ear. They can get over the wall easily enough but not into the house. I'll take the first watch tonight."

Night had suddenly dropped down, as it does in the tropics; there was always with the night a kind of subtle threat that seemed to come from the land as if it didn't like civilization, as if it only waited to take back its own.

None of the club came that night, but we didn't bother to take watches. Richard made himself a kind of bed in the living room, and I tried to sleep in the once-attractive pink and white and green guest room. Actually, though, we prowled around most of the night and drank coffee. By morning there was no ducking the fact that if we had made a trap, then we ourselves were caught in it.

It was another sunny, calm day, blue sky overhead, glossy green leaves everywhere and the fountain bubbling cozily in the little pool, which I tried to clear of its débris from the hurricane. Once Richard went to the gate again. "I'll just see if somebody is out there . . ." The silk hat sat rakishly on top of a heap of dead twigs and leaves we had stacked together. He picked it up, put it on a branch, opened the gate and shoved out the hat. After scarcely a second, something spat viciously again from across the street. Richard banged the gate and bolted it. He had dropped the hat outside. "Damn fool," he said. "Didn't even wait to see if somebody was under the hat."

"Didn't wait to wonder why anybody would wear a silk hat here and now," I said and cleared dead leaves from the tiny pool, disturbing a frog who hopped out wildly; I lost what composure I had and squealed.

It seemed very strange to be that near a big city, with policemen and every kind of law-enforcing agency, and yet to be totally helpless, marooned as if on a desert island because there was no telephone, and because somebody with a gun waited and watched from his hiding place across the street. Late in the afternoon, though, two telephone repairmen came; they drove up to the gate in a truck and nobody took a shot at it. Richard opened the gate, and one of them told him that a woman who said she was the maid had reported that the telephone was out of order. Oh, dear Bessie, I thought. One of the men held up the battered, muddy silk hat and looked puzzled. "You never know what you'll find rolling around after a hurricane. This hat's got a funny-looking hole in it." He held up the hat toward the sunlight so we could all see the hole. "Looks as if a bullet made it." Both gave us thoughtful looks.

Richard said, "It does, doesn't it? The phone is this way," and led them into the house.

After some coming and going through the gate and the patio, both men left. They were thoughtful, for the telephone wire had not been torn down by the hurricane; it had been neatly sawed through in back of the wall outside the kitchen.

They had repaired it. But at the gate again one of them turned to Richard. "See here. I take it there's been no trouble here? No attempted burglary? Anything of the kind?"

Richard hesitated for a bare second and I could almost see what flashed through his mind. Here was help. We were not, after all, in a trap we had made, cut off from any sort of aid. On the other hand, it could still become a trap for Dino—or the tiger. He said, "I suppose anything can happen in a storm. But, no, things are all right."

So the men went away. Richard waited until he heard the sound of their truck before he bolted the gate. Then he looked at me. "We could have asked for the police. We could have got away."

"It wouldn't change anything."

"Actually it might make it more dangerous. That is—well, here we know, in a way, what to expect. At home we wouldn't."

I thought of the rambling Lowry house, providing a hundred hiding places for a tiger; each hiding place Dino would know. I thought of perhaps driving to the village or walking along a country road and meeting murder.

Richard said contrarily, "All the same, this was a poor idea of mine. It's not going to work and I wish you were out of this place."

Again I was tense and snappish. "For a man who thinks he's very logical you change your mind too often."

Unexpectedly, he laughed. "One thing I haven't changed my mind about, although she can be very trying. Come on, let's have some drinks and then we'll eat. Good old Gil. He keeps plenty of liquor and plenty of food on hand."

"I suppose it's because they live so far from town." I wished they lived right in the middle of a city.

"Very dangerous," George Hobson had said.

It was one of the times when I was sure that we had been wrong to stay on in the house in the faint hope of Dino's return and probably the fainter hope of inducing him to give up whatever it was that he was involved in. Richard felt as I did, for he mixed a gin and tonic, sipped it and said, "That damn letter. They think they've got to have it and they know that we've read it and know whatever is in the letter. I've got to get you out of here somehow."

"If it's drug traffic . . ."

"I know. I've got to make sure before we do anything about it."

We had dinner, the swift tropic twilight came down like a curtain and we were still going around in the same circles of conjecture. We were in the living room, with the dampish patches where there had been blood on the rug, when the telephone rang.

FOURTEEN

We both ran to answer it. Richard took the hall telephone, said hello and motioned me to the kitchen, meaning the kitchen extension. When I got there and put it to my ear, I heard a man speaking in a hurried voice. ". . . draw the line at murder. That fellow in Hong Kong was in on it. He ratted. I'm about to do the same thing."

"Who is this?" Richard said.

"You don't know me. That is, you have the list. I'm on it. My name—but it's not my name."

"How can I reach you?"

"I'll see to that. I've made some money on it, but it's too great a risk. I've been a law-abiding citizen up to—well, this is outside the law and I knew it. But I'll have nothing to do with murder. Can I trust you?"

"With what?"

"Not to give me away to the law, of course!" His voice sounded impatient.

Richard didn't answer. I broke in. "Promise him, Dick. Promise him—"

The voice changed a little. "Who's that?"

"I'm Dino's wife," I cried. "I don't want to go to the police about Dino. I only want him to stop anything that is, as you say, outside the law. Anything you tell me, I promise not to tell the police—"

There was a click and then the dial tone. Richard came in as I stood staring at the telephone.

"One of the men on the list!" I cried. "It's too much for him—"

"And 'Hobson ratted.' Well, we knew that. Now it's too much for Mr. Whatever-his-real-name-is. He wasn't above making money in some obviously illegal way but he's scared of murder. He'll come here."

"If he comes here, they'll kill him!" This seemed as bizarre, as incredible a statement as the knife left so casually on the table in my room had seemed incredible, yet there it had been.

"Presumably this guy knew what he got into in the beginning. He knows the whole plan, whatever it is. He said he's made money . . ." I thought of all the money in Dino's wallet.

Richard thought of it too. "Whatever it is, Dino has already got enough money out of it to go around with his wallet full of bills. Probably has more somewhere, must have. Yet the plan—the conspiracy can't have gone on for very long. Hobson would have sent a warning to Mr. Lowry soon after he learned of it. Somehow, of course, they—or Dino—got Hobson into the thing. Dino knew him obviously by way of old Mr. Chen. I think that Hobson was supposed to be some kind of—I don't know—middleman perhaps. Receiver of goods. I feel that Hobson didn't string along with them for very long. In a few minutes maybe we'll know just what it is about. Then we can do whatever is necessary."

"If it's dope smuggling . . ." I said again.

"We'll try to find out where Dino is. How to get in touch with him. Perhaps this man will tell us."

"Then what?"

"We can give Dino a chance to go to the authorities, I suppose. Tell them the whole thing."

"Turn state's evidence—is that what you call it?"

"Close enough. We'll cross that bridge when or if we reach it. All we can do now is wait."

So we waited and listened for any betraying rattle at a shutter. We also listened for the man who had telephoned us. Yet surely, I said once, he wouldn't be fool enough to come to that house, under the eyes of his confreres, who might suspect his planned defection.

"On the other hand," Richard said, "he wouldn't be fool enough to let Dino or anybody know that he was about to rat, as he says."

"If he felt he had to tell us all he knows, then he must have regard for—well, law and decency and . . ."

Richard gave me a look refuting any such motive. "This man is not decent, as Hobson was. He's made some money, he's out on a limb through making that money and he wants to make a gesture which might help. He's going to tell me and you the whole affair, so that when it comes to the attention of an officer of the law he can say in honesty something like 'I didn't realize just what this was all about; as soon as I did realize it I took steps to stop it. Ask Mrs. Lowry. Ask

Blake. They'll tell you that I made a clean breast of the whole thing.' "

"And the police will say, 'Why didn't you come to us?' "

Richard thought that over and, unexpectedly, widely yawned. "Maybe. Let's turn on all the lights so that if he gets up the nerve to come here, he'll think all is well."

"Unless he's shot when he rings the gate bell," I said morosely.

As it happened, Richard made some kind of move which sent a glass ashtray crashing to the terrazzo floor and I jumped three feet; at least it felt like three feet but probably wasn't. Richard began to scoop up the splinters of glass and I just stood and stared at the spots on the rug where we'd tried to wash off the blood and which still looked rusty, and said at last, "We'll never come here for a honeymoon, never. Even if we ever have a honeymoon."

Richard dropped the pieces of glass in a wastebasket. "I'm running up quite a claim for damages from Gil. We'll have that honeymoon, believe me . . ."

I jumped again, for there was the peremptory blowing of an automobile horn somewhere outside the patio, in the street.

"It can't be—" Richard ran into the hall and opened the door. I followed. He turned on the two floodlights in the patio, artfully arranged to give a romantic kind of glow to the pool and the tiny fountain. The lights were also bright enough to see that nobody was hiding among the bamboos or the bougainvilleae or around the big water oak. The gate bell kept on ringing in short, shrill stabs.

Richard shouted, "Who's that?"

A voice wailed from behind the gate. "Let me in! I've got to phone! There's a dead man in my cab."

Neither of us thought for a second that it might have been a ruse to permit one of the club to get into the house, and it wasn't. Richard opened the gate and a cabdriver burst in. "Like a stuck pig!" he wailed. "All over everything. Where's a phone . . ." He pulled a blue bandanna out of a hip pocket, mopped his face and half sobbed, "Look at him. Just take a look. I couldn't do it myself; it made me sick. Maybe he's not dead . . ."

I could see the cab, which had pulled up very close to the gate. The rear door was open and the lights in the cab were on. I could see only that the man slumped on the floor was bulky, dressed in brown. His feet were at a strange angle, turned over so I could see brilliantly polished tan shoes. Then Richard came between and leaned into the cab.

No shot came from anywhere. I didn't even think of it at that moment. Richard finally stood up straight, slammed the door shut and came back inside the patio. He closed and bolted the gate. The cabdriver mopped his glistening face. "He's dead, mister. Isn't he?"

"Yes; we'll phone for the police."

The driver clutched Richard's arm. "You talk to them, mister. Tell them I didn't have anything to do with it. Tell them this guy just got in my cab and gave me this address."

"This number? Are you sure?"

"Well, I—no. The fact is, I knew it was this street but I wasn't sure of the number, couldn't remember it, see. Often happens like that, so I turned around to ask him and there he was. Like a stuck pig." He began to sob, actually, loud and frightened sobs, and babbled, "They had me up only last week. The judge said next time he'd give me ten days. They let me off with a fine but . . ." He gave a wild swipe at his face and shouted at Richard, "I wasn't drunk last week, not really. Just had a couple, you tell them. Tell them I'm not drunk tonight. Tell them—"

"All right. I'll do the talking."

They went into the house, although the cabdriver gave a harried look at the gate as if he wanted to run, leave his cab, leave anything, but most of all leave a dead man who had obviously been murdered.

Richard was talking to the police on the phone. Apparently whomever he spoke to wanted to talk to the cabdriver, and Richard said he'd had a shock but was right there, in the house. After a moment he said, "Yes . . . all right," and hung up, and the cabdriver clutched his arm again. "What'd he say?"

"It was the desk sergeant—said he'd send over a prowl car. Want a drink? No, I guess you'd better not. Well, then, sit down and try to pull yourself together. Was this man alone when he got into the cab?"

"Yes . . ." The cabdriver collapsed suddenly and miserably on the small telephone chair, which creaked. "He didn't kill himself. Not like that." He gave a shudder, so that his fat legs, bulging over the small chair, quivered. "No. Throat's cut from ear to ear."

I decided to go into the living room and sit down. The

lights were on and the room was bright and attractive, with its white rugs and walls and its gay red and green and orange cushions, but I hated it. Against all that brightness I could see George Hobson lying stretched out on the tattered piece of red silk behind his dusty counter. I could even see the Coromandel screen across the back of the little shop and smell the sandalwood and mustiness. I could also see a knife casually left on a table in my room. At the same time I could hear Richard and the cabdriver.

"Who killed him then?" Richard said, but rather as if he were asking himself.

The cabdriver had stopped his shocked, spasmodic sobbing. "I sure didn't. Never had such a shock in my life. There he was, getting into the cab, giving me an address—on this street but damned if I can remember the number. You weren't expecting him, mister?"

"No," Richard said flatly.

I thought, But we *were* expecting him.

Richard said, very quietly, "Where did you pick up this man?"

"Corner of Marle and Elwell. There's a motor court nearby and a drugstore. He hailed me. Looked all right, in a hurry maybe, but all right. Look here, mister—" There was a very slight pause; the driver's voice changed a little, becoming rather sly. "Maybe somebody got into my cab at one of those traffic lights and killed the guy?"

"Who?" Richard said bluntly.

"Well, I only mean—Well, *I* didn't kill him."

There was another pause. Then Richard asked, "What exactly did you hear?"

"Nothing! Nothing—"

"What did you see? You've got a rear-view mirror. What did you see?"

"Not a thing. Honest, I don't know anything."

"If you'd heard a moan or a scuffle or anything of the kind, you'd have turned around and looked. Wouldn't you?"

The cabdriver sounded defiant. "All depends! Some fares I wouldn't turn around and look at if all hell broke loose. Drunks, say. Or if a stickup man got into my cab, I'd tell him to take my money and leave. I'd tell him I hadn't even seen him. I couldn't identify him. It don't pay, mister, to see too much."

"So you don't intend to tell the whole story," Richard said.

The cabdriver began to bluster. "See here, mister, that man

was killed. Somebody killed him. I'm not about to stick my neck out, or my throat!"

"You know more than you're telling me, then. The police will get it out of you. You might as well tell me."

"The police ain't going to get anything out of me I don't want to tell them. Besides"—the voice grew sly again and cunning—"I haven't said I saw anything or know anything, and I'll tell you the truth, mister—I didn't know the guy was killed. That I didn't know till I got outside your gate."

"But if nobody got into the cab, then who killed him?"

"I—sure, I know the police will ask, 'Who killed him? Who got into the cab?' Sure, I'll say I thought somebody got in but I didn't hear a word, maybe some talk but nothing else. I'll say I heard the door slam when somebody got out again, I'll say that—"

"When you get ready to talk, let me know what really happened, will you? I'll make it worth your while," Richard said coolly and came into the living room, crossed quickly to me and gave me a wallet and a handful of small papers. "Get rid of them," he said so low that I could scarcely hear it, and went back to the cabdriver. Richard had clearly taken the wallet and papers from the man in the cab while he leaned inside for that long, long moment.

Get rid of them. The police were on their way. So I must hurry, hide them—but where? It's extremely difficult to think, on the spur of the moment, of a hiding place with a chance of escaping the search by the police, who know every trick of hide-and-seek. I went through the little hall and into my room.

It was all serene and tidy; I had gathered up the contents of my handbag which had been scattered on the floor. Richard had replaced the knife in the kitchen. There was no place to hide anything. The bathroom was orderly, neat, and there was no place to hide anything there. Then I thought of the kitchen, went into it and found a hiding place. I opened the freezer, took out a package—of peas, I think—carefully opened it without tearing the paper and shoved the frozen contents down the incinerator. I put the wallet and papers in the package, resealed it as best I could and stacked it back in the freezer. I heard Richard coming through the dining room. ". . . a drink of cold water won't hurt you," he called back to the cabdriver and came in as I was closing the freezer.

"In there?"

I nodded.

Richard said, "He was Mr. John Smith of San Francisco."

The scared rabbit who had run from us when Blondie touched his arm. The scared rabbit who had nearly had a heart attack when he read Richard's telegram. The scared rabbit who had every reason to be frightened. I felt a sharp kind of pity for the scared rabbit. "Are you sure?"

"Oh, yes. I didn't have time to look at the stuff I took from his pockets. I just snatched what I could find."

"Then he was the one who phoned. What are we going to tell the police?"

"I don't know. I do think that Dino must know of this murder and he'll get out here as fast as he can. There's no point in our staying here. So I'm going to take you home to—some place where you'll be safe. We can't leave now, for the police would know it and have every reason to wonder about it, hold us, question us." He gave an odd little sigh. "I always thought of myself as a law-abiding citizen. It's not fair to the police to let it go like this. It is deliberately concealing evidence. But I can't see anything else to do."

"What are you going to do when we get home? Dino will never go there."

"Call Inspector Filladon, I think. Get some quiet legal advice. I tell you," he said wearily, "I'm the wrong kind of lawyer. Now, if I were a criminal lawyer, I'd know exactly what to do. Maybe."

The cabdriver called from the hall, pleading, "Hey, mister —here they are. Please, mister!"

FIFTEEN

The police didn't stay long but they stayed too long. They didn't search the house and didn't even glance at the freezer, but they did take a deliberate look around every room. They did try to get the cabdriver to remember what house number his fare had given him, but he couldn't remember. He insisted that he had turned around to ask his fare the number and that was when he saw him. "Like a stuck pig," the cabdriver repeated and I wished that he would use some less hideous phrase. He also stated, quite blithely really, that he felt sure someone had got into the cab at a stop light, but he hadn't turned to look.

"You mean you didn't collect another fare?" one of the policemen asked skeptically.

"I was concentrating on the driving," the cabdriver said loftily. "Had my mind on business. Then I drive up here and turn around to ask about the house number and—"

"Yes, you told us."

They talked about the fact that they had found no wallet and apparently assumed that the murderer had stolen it. However, they asked me, and Richard, if we knew the murdered man and we both said flatly, "No, we don't even know his name," which was the letter of the truth, for his name was certainly not John Smith; but it was not the essence of the truth, it was the kind of small ruse which can and often does contribute to a very big lie.

They asked if we had expected him and Richard said no, and did not add that we had expected someone. They seemed to know something of Gil Rayburn, and were inclined to be polite and even friendly when they discovered that Richard and Gil were old friends and that we were staying there at Gil's invitation. Up to then I think they had been a little doubtful about this strange man and woman cozily installed in Gil's house.

They didn't ask why we happened to be there at a time when our host and his wife were away, but Richard volunteered the information: he said that Gil expected to be home in a few days but probably had been delayed by the storm. Both policemen nodded.

There were a great many other questions but none that implied any particular interest in us. They seemed to accept the cabdriver's explanation; they also seemed to think that he might have been drinking and possibly was not in a state to give them a very clear report.

By that time there were two more cars outside the gate. I could see lights, for the gate was now open, and hear voices. After a time the taxi was driven away by the police; I saw it leave with its unfortunate passenger still in the back, hunched over on the floor. When the police left they took the cabdriver with them; he did not seem to relish his escort.

I glanced around the patio. We had cleared up all the rubbish from the hurricane; it was charming again, tranquil, its green foliage touched with silver from the floodlights, its little fountain bubbling away cheerfully—and I was afraid of it. I was afraid of the house.

It had been so attractive, the house had seemed almost an enchanted spot in its beauty, the way its low roof snuggled down beneath the enormous water oak, the green paths of the patio, the light colors inside the house, my own wide, airy room with its green chaise longue and curtains and the camellia pink border around the white rug—oh, a charming room and murder might have found me there.

But the house had changed. I felt obscurely ashamed, as if I had brought something into the house which might take up residence there. Now I only wanted to leave it.

"Let's give them a little time, be sure they are gone," Richard said. "Then we'll call a cab and go to the airport and get the next flight to New York. First, though, Smith's wallet . . ."

So we got it out of the freezer and found that it was conspicuously bare of anything like identification: no credit cards, no bank card, no driver's license, nothing. There was some money, about three hundred dollars. There was nothing at all to indicate Mr. Smith's real name.

The scraps of paper gave no information whatever, being composed of impersonal items: timetables showing the ferry schedules between San Francisco and Oakland, a battered matchbook, rate cards for a car rental service.

"Clearly, whoever got into the cab at some traffic light—which sounds likely—didn't want money," Richard said. "He took only things that might identify Smith. His object was to kill Smith, remove identification and get away."

He shoveled together the wallet and the papers, put them in his pocket and went to the telephone. I listened while he called the airport and asked about flights to New York.

"It's all right," Richard said, putting down the telephone. "We've got plenty of time. I think we'd better stay here as long as we can, in the event some policeman thinks of something else he wants to question us about. Or a police car might be cruising around. Better get your things together, though."

I had started toward my room when the telephone rang. I heard Richard say, "Are you sure? . . . Did he see him clearly? I must know a number of men who fit that general description but . . . No, I can't think of anyone who would be coming here to see me . . . Thank you. I'll get in touch if anything occurs to me."

He came back. "It was a police lieutenant. He says that when the cabdriver took a close look at the—at Mr. Smith, he began to stammer and backtrack. Said he wasn't even sure that the murdered man was his passenger. Apparently he began to describe somebody else but he didn't make sense. The police officer thinks the cabdriver is so scared that he's inventing a description that might fit anybody. He's afraid of being a witness.

"He said he wouldn't look around no matter what happened in the cab. And he was so afraid that he actually sobbed."

Richard thought for a moment. "What it adds up to is that the driver is lying as fast as he can and getting himself mixed up. The police seem to feel that he's afraid positively to identify anybody at all. There's just one thing they can depend on and that is that he had a dead man in his cab! But it does look as if the murderer had some reason to guess that the rabbit intended to see us. So he followed the cab, probably in another taxi, jumped out of that and into the cab with the rabbit. The murderer could be anyone on that list of names. We don't know the identity of a single man on it. There's San Francisco—murdered. There's Jones—ugly, thin, dark, Tampa. There's a man in Chicago and a man in New York. There's Dino. And Blondie. And not a scrap of real evidence anywhere."

The gate bell rang suddenly. For a second I was sure that

the police had returned and perhaps had discovered some evidence linking us with the murder of the scared rabbit.

Richard went to answer it. I heard him call cautiously through the gate, "Who is it?"

A woman replied. She was a friend of Mrs. Rayburn's, she said. She lived down the street. She had seen the police cars and hoped there was no trouble.

Richard opened the gate. Blondie walked in.

I didn't know it was Blondie until she was actually in the house and even then I was not entirely sure of it.

The floodlights in the patio showed her clearly. She was wearing orange-colored shorts and a red shirt, and no gun could possibly have been concealed on that sleek, plump figure. Her legs were rather stocky; she should never have dared wearing shorts. Her hair was black, cut very short, and sleek too; she wore no glasses. She brushed past us and into the house, for Richard and I were transfixed, staring at her, both of us trying to decide whether or not she was what she said she was. Her eyes were an intense, jewel-like blue, the blue of a Siamese cat's eyes. It even seemed to me that as with a Siamese cat when he's a little agitated, there was a faint garnet glow to her eyes. She glanced around very swiftly, yet somehow covertly.

"I saw the police cars," she said again.

I had heard only a few words spoken by the maid in Hong Kong. Richard had heard only a few words over the telephone in San Francisco. Her voice was crisp, the words very slightly tinged with a British accent, but I couldn't be sure that it was Blondie. I said, "Mrs. Rayburn isn't here." It was not much to say.

"Oh, I know," she said. "I'm Mrs. Larker. I live down the street." Her eyes shifted around rapidly, looking for somebody or something. I edged farther from her and Richard, behind her, saw it and said with his lips, "Blondie?"

I couldn't be sure. I shook my head a little.

But she was plumpish. She was, in an odd way, attractive. I wanted her to talk more, hoping that I might be able to identify something about her.

Richard said, "There was a street accident. The cabdriver came here to make a phone call. How nice of you to come and ask."

If it was Blondie it was not nice at all. She turned to him, and her Siamese-cat eyes glinted with that lovely jewel blue.

She said, "Who was hurt? Was he badly injured? Where is he?"

"I don't know really," Richard replied, taking it in his stride. "They hauled him off. How did you make out with the hurricane?"

"The—oh, the hurricane." She had no handbag. That fact seemed to attest to her being a neighbor. But then she dug a handkerchief from a pocket of her shirt and the faintest whiff of Chanel Number Five floated toward me. All my senses sprang to attention as if an alarm had rung. She paused, the handkerchief at her nose, and said, nasally through it, as if she guessed our doubts and wished to disguise her voice, something like "Dreadful cold. Can hardly speak. Was the injured man killed?"

The whiff of fragrance was not convincing. But the lithe movement of her plump hand was like that of the hand which had swiftly closed my suitcase in Hong Kong. Then I saw a queerly stubby, short thumb. So I nodded at Richard. He waited a fraction of a second to be sure I meant it, and then simply reached out and caught the woman by the neck, his hands around her throat.

She didn't scream. That was very odd.

She didn't struggle. That was odd, too.

So Richard relaxed his grip.

She didn't try to jerk away. Instead, like a cat again, she relaxed completely, leaning against Richard. He caught her arms instinctively to keep her from falling. She then lashed out at him with one of those sturdy legs and gave a twist to Richard's neck with those plump and strong hands but Richard pulled back, wrested away from her and then caught her arm as she sprang for the door. It was over in a split second. This time he held her with her arms locked behind her and nodded at me to lock the door, which I did.

"Get the revolver," he told me. "I put it in a drawer before the police came. In the dining room."

I ran for the dining room and found the revolver, wedged down into the Rayburn flat silver. When I came back, Richard had shoved Blondie into the living room. He held on to one of her arms, also rather stocky and thick, while he held out his other hand for the gun, which I gave him.

"All right," he said then to Blondie. "Now, why did you come here?"

Her eyes were truly red and shifted rapidly around the room. The lights were stronger there. Her face had the indefinable look of the East which the maid in Hong Kong had had, yet it was neither Chinese nor Indian, Asian or Caucasian. Oddly I felt a little sorry for her; somehow her face, her character, seemed to have sprung from nothing and to have no destination. It was a mistaken impression, a fleeting impression, but there it was and for a second I wished that Richard would release his hard grip on her arm. She said, "This is terrible, to treat me like this. I'm a neighbor. I came to inquire. You had an accident. I saw the police. Where is he? Was the man killed?"

"How did you know anybody was injured?"

"I—I saw the ambulance—"

"There wasn't any ambulance. There were only police cars. Who are you?"

"I'm Mrs. Marker . . . from down the street. A neighbor. I came to inquire. You can't treat me like this—"

"You said Mrs. Larker the first time," Richard said. "Come off it, Blondie—whatever your name is. You followed us from Hong Kong. You want Hobson's letter."

"I tell you I'm a neighbor." A glint of blue, calm and serene returned to her eyes. "If you don't believe me, use the telephone."

But the serene blue in Blondie's eyes warned Richard. It didn't warn me. I only thought that in setting a trap for a tiger we had snared a savage and dangerous kitten.

But Richard said, "Lock the door, Marcia. Then try the phone."

I guessed then, locked the front door quickly and lifted the telephone. As I expected, there was no dial tone. It was entirely dead. Richard said, "Wires cut again." He leveled his gun at Blondie. "I should tell you that I'm a good shot."

She smiled openly. She also purred. "You wouldn't shoot a woman, Mr. Blake. You couldn't possibly shoot me."

And of course he couldn't. And, of course, he knew he couldn't.

Blondie smiled; she was smug and triumphant. She really purred, almost literally. "So now give me the Hobson letter. You see, the men who are associated with me are not very nice men. To put it clearly, they're very dangerous men. They want that letter. Neither you nor your"—she gave me a glance of calm, blue contempt—"woman will be safe until you give us the Hobson letter. No matter where you go, no matter what you do, your lives won't be worth that much." She snapped a finger against a stubby thumb. "They—these men will never give up."

"But we know what is in the Hobson letter," Richard said quietly.

"You haven't gone to the police. That's clear. You are not going to go to the police. Oh, no, not you," she purred. "And I know why. You have a very tender conscience, Mr. Blake. You didn't want to turn Dino over to the police—not because you were once friends, oh, no—but because you're trying to take his—this woman. You feel guilty. Perhaps"—she shrugged—"perhaps you have even felt that you should help Dino, turn him aside from—that is, bring him home again. It's all very clear to me. That's why you didn't give the letter to the police in Hong Kong. You couldn't bring yourself to injure Dino. You feel guilty, so—" She laughed and purred at the same time, which doesn't seem likely but it sounded like it. "But soon you will conquer your conscience. Soon you will go to the police. Oh, I understand you."

Richard looked at her curiously, as if she belonged to some new and strange breed. "That's one way of looking at it," he said mildly. "I can't honestly say that that particular view ever occurred to me."

"So give me the letter and the list now. You have them here, in the house. We'll find them, but it'll be easier if you give them to me now. And then you'll never hear any more of any of us. I promise . . ."

"But, you see," Richard said mildly again, "as I told you, we know what's in the letter. Aren't you afraid that I will, as you say, conquer my conscience and tell the police everything?"

The faintest red glow came up into her eyes, but she still smiled. "But the letter and the list are evidence. You can *say* anything you like. Who is going to believe you? Now give me the letter and the list and I'll leave."

"Your friends are just outside, aren't they?" Richard said. "They sent you in here to find out exactly what happened to the man in the taxi."

"What did happen?" she flashed, like a cat pouncing upon a mouse.

Then I heard something, I couldn't have said what, but something at the hall door. I knew that someone was there. This time the wall and the gate had been an insufficient barrier. Richard heard it too and gave a rather wistful look at the revolver in his hand. But Blondie was right; he couldn't possibly have shot her. He said, "Marcia, I think I saw some kind of rope in the toolroom."

I ran through the dining room and kitchen; in the little furnace- and tool-room—where someone had hidden most uncomfortably, it struck me, but with intent to kill me if necessary—I found what Richard called a rope but which was in fact merely a thin clothesline, neatly coiled up on a kind of standard. I rolled out some of it, got a kitchen knife to cut it with and sawed through what proved to be a surprisingly tough, if slender, line.

Someone pounded on the door as I ran through the hall and I hoped the lock would hold. I handed the rope to Richard and he took it, gave me the gun and eyed Blondie as if he loathed his task. "I really don't know what else to do with her," he said to me. I thought that he could no more tie her up securely than he could have shot at her.

I had no qualms at all. So I said firmly, "I'll do it."

But I couldn't. The instant Blondie saw me take the rope from Richard and hand him back the gun, she knew that I didn't have Richard's scruples. She flung herself at me, fighting, struggling, kicking and trying to trip me with those stocky legs. I fought back but she knocked me off balance, my head hit the corner of the big glass table and I remember merely sinking down into a kind of fuzzy blackness. It didn't last long, that moment of unconsciousness. But when I opened my eyes, sat up and felt a little dizzy, Richard was knotting the rope around her wrists and ankles and she was struggling against him in what looked like a frenzy of terror. It was as if for some reason a rope was particularly terrifying to her. She screamed, "Not a rope—not a rope—"

I got up on the sofa and then to my feet. Richard saw me and said, "Get the gun. On the table."

I picked up the gun. Richard finished knotting the thin rope around her squirming wrists. She had scratched his face, raking fingernails across it. One of his eyes was already red and swelling. Whoever pounded at the door kept on pounding, loudly now.

Blondie began to squall, thin and high like an angry cat, and Dino shouted, through it all, "Marcia, open the door! Marcia, open the door!"

Richard took the gun from me and wiped at the bloody streak on his cheek where Blondie's fingernails had got him. Blondie stopped writhing and squalling and began to bite at the rope around her wrists. Her plump face had turned a kind of ashy gray; she chewed and bit in such a frenzy that I suddenly felt sorry for her; I almost wanted to let her go.

Richard knew it. Perhaps he felt as I did. He said, however, shortly, "She's all right. Nothing else to do. Don't touch her, Marcia." He went to the hall and shouted to Dino, "Your girl friend is here. She can't help you. I've got a gun. I want to talk to you."

We didn't talk to Dino. Richard didn't open the door and let him in, for at that point the club made a mistake. Two men began to talk to Dino.

They were quite distinct, the two strange voices and Dino's voice. An argument seemed to be going on. But the point was that there were three men out there.

Blondie stopped chewing to listen.

Richard leaned close to the door. The mumble of voices seemed to fade a little. Suddenly Richard thrust the gun into my hand. "They're making for the French doors to your room. Those doors won't hold." He ran toward his room.

I held the gun. By now I couldn't hear the men outside. Blondie looked at me and I looked at Blondie. It seems strange now but suddenly I said, "I'm really sorry about the ropes."

It also seems strange that she said, "They used to tie me and then leave me and—But you'd never know. Not in your sheltered life."

It was all I could do to keep from going over to her and loosening the ropes. But then I heard a kind of thump and thud from the direction of my bedroom. Richard came running from his bedroom. He had his gray summer suit draped over one arm, with trousers and sleeves of the coat dangling. He took the revolver and without a glance at Blondie pulled me after him, through the hall, where the banging on the French doors to my room was ominously louder, and into the master bedroom. "I hope there's a key," he said and turned on the lights. There was one, and he locked the door. Then he ran to a window, opened it and flung back the shutters. The pounding outside my room was furious. Richard gave me a wry, half-laughing yet serious glance and said, "There's a time to retreat and this is it. Get a dress out of the closet. Hurry!" After I had snatched something out of the closet that looked like a dress, Richard pushed me through the window and came out after me.

It was dark and warm. From my bedroom we heard a final crash and clatter. We ran into the hot darkness, through some spiky kind of shrubbery. We ran, stumbling, groping our way.

SIXTEEN

❀❀❀

I thought that Richard had some idea of getting to the back of the neighboring house, for we were running in that direction.

I remember saying, jerkily, panting, that it wouldn't help. "Nobody's there. The phone will have been disconnected."

At least I thought I said that. I do remember Richard whispering, "Don't talk . . ."

We made such a racket crashing through the masses of shrubbery that it seemed to me they must hear us from the low white house we had left, and which I caught one glimpse of, ghostly in the starlight. At once it vanished again behind a long line of shrubs, black and thick.

We didn't reach the house next door; we had veered too far to the left. Without any warning we came out into a street. There were lampposts, but the road seemed to be an even more remote part of the development which had not developed. It stretched emptily away, grass growing along the narrow pavement, the streetlights only emphasizing its desolation. There may have been houses somewhere, hidden by foliage, but there were no visible lights except from those rather ghostly lampposts at long intervals.

Richard seemed to pause to get his bearings. Then he took my hand and we ran down the road again. I was wearing my new denim sneakers, and Richard a pair of tennis shoes he had taken from Gil's room. Our feet made eerie, soft thuds along the vacant street. I began to feel as if we were at the end of nowhere, pursued by nothing we could see, and with no definite goal, no place of safety.

Suddenly Richard stopped and drew me into the shadow of a dense thicket which softly scratched my bare arms and legs. "They'll search the house first, I think. They'll try to find the letter. They don't know which direction we took. There are only three of them. Four with Blondie. They can't watch the whole neighborhood. Now, put on the dress. Hurry!"

111

He struggled into his business suit, but I slid the dress over my shorts and shirt easily, since it was quite large.

If anybody had been watching when we came out into the street again, we would have seemed quite different, Richard in his ordinary summer worsted, I in Miz Rayburn's dress which was hanging down to my knees. Richard kept looking behind us. I looked too; no shadow was moving, nothing was moving along the street.

We turned a corner and all at once, without warning, the streetlights stopped. In another moment the paved street stopped too. Before us stretched a narrow road, dimly seen, probably rarely traveled.

I caught my breath, painfully, my throat burning. Richard said, "Look. That must be the city. We'll go in that direction."

I looked and saw the faintest pinkish glow off in the distance but hadn't any idea in which direction—north, south, or what.

Then we both saw the headlights of a car coming slowly along the paved and lighted street behind us, deliberately hunting us down.

Richard whirled me around, off the road, into the dense shrubbery, and we stumbled along over sandy soil and branches that tripped and caught us. The headlights were coming nearer. We could now hear the low throb of the car's engine. I lost Richard.

He had let go my hand for a moment; only later did I learn that he was pulling out the gun, which he had wedged into his belt. It happened in a second; I had got an unbearable amount of sand in my sneaker; in sheer automatic reflex I bent down, took it off, shook out the sand and reached for Richard and he wasn't there. He wasn't anywhere.

I didn't dare call him, for I could no longer hear the car and I knew it must have stopped. I couldn't see the headlights now, but I could see a glow from somewhere beyond the thickets of shrubs.

I groped around with my hands. There was nothing but bamboos and palmettos and all of them gave forth betraying rustles when I touched them, so I stopped and crouched down, thrusting myself into some bamboos. After a moment they stopped quivering and rustling. There was only my heavy breathing and the hard thumps of my heart.

But I was lost or Richard was lost; it was the same thing. I told myself I must not panic, I must not run in circles. I must stay exactly where I was. I listened for another rustle. Richard must look for me. He must make some sound. He couldn't call for me. He mustn't speak. I mustn't speak.

There wasn't any sound at all except for that heavy thud of my heart. Then the bamboos shook and quivered just a little around me; I thought that Richard was close, looking for me. I was still very quiet but I had to make certain. I parted some of the bamboos very cautiously, very gently, and it wasn't Richard at all; it was Dino standing just outside the fringe of reeds, listening. I could see his handsome profile vaguely in the starlight; I could see the outline of his fuzzy beard. I knew the set of his shoulders and the way he bent his head when he was listening.

Then I was afraid of Dino.

He waited and waited. In the distance a man shouted to somebody else, not urgently, rather as if the two were merely keeping a check on each other. I couldn't hear the words. Then Dino shouted, "Spread out a little. They've got to be here somewhere—"

A car started up with a roar and two men shouted, "Stop them!" "Stop them, they've got the car!" Somebody yelled, "You damn fool, you left the keys in the car!"

There was the crashing sound of feet plunging through the sand and shrubs. Dino stayed perfectly still, exactly where he was, almost as if he had an instinct for tracking me. I watched his dark profile until my eyes began to ache. The shouts of the other two men grew fainter. Dino remained motionless, except when he turned his head just a fraction, listening for me.

I wondered which of us would give up first. The sound of the car was diminishing rapidly. For a moment I couldn't hear it at all. I did hear a shot. There was no mistaking that sound; my experience with revolver shots had been limited but I knew what it was. I didn't know what had happened.

Richard had had Gil's gun; I remembered vaguely that he had stuck it into his belt. I didn't doubt that the men with Dino could have had guns.

Somebody in the club liked knives.

Dino must have heard the revolver shot too; he couldn't have missed it in that silent and deserted strip of sand and patchy thickets. I could see him turn a little to listen, perhaps to watch. But he stayed there. I couldn't hear the other men at all now. I supposed that they had pursued the car. Richard would come back for me. I hoped I had not strayed too far in that warm darkness from the place where we had lost each other.

Dino suddenly moved a little, crouched down and was very still as if, again, he had heard something. Then his black silhouette moved away slightly, stealthily.

I didn't move. I had a queer notion that he had merely crept around the edge of some clump of palmettos and was waiting for me to emerge from wherever I had hidden.

I waited and waited. He didn't come back.

After a long time I thought I heard a faint rustle, then a quick, instantly muffled grunt, and then nothing at all. So I waited and listened and finally heard Richard, whispering through the night, "Marcia . . . Marcia."

I didn't know where he was, but I knew it was Richard. I parted the bamboos and they rustled and Richard's hand came out of the night and touched my face.

"All right? Come on—" At that moment there was a tremendous wham of air which shook the bamboos and the whole world; it was instantly followed by a roar of staggering sound and flame that lighted up the vacant land of bamboos and palmettos and scrub pines. Richard was kneeling down, reaching for me.

The echoes of the roar and explosion died down but the red-and-orange light spread higher. "It's all right," Richard said. "It's their gas tank—I thought it would never go up. Come on. There seems to be a factory on a main street nearby."

I crawled out, this time holding tightly to his hand. "Dino was here . . ."

"I know. I knocked him out. He's over there somewhere."

"Where's the car? What did you do? What happened?" The red glare in the sky was leaping wildly, sending up black clouds.

"Stole their car. Stopped it up the road. Shot a hole in the gas tank. Threw a lighted matchbook where I thought the gasoline would leak, and ran for it. I must have misjudged the spot. It took longer than I expected. But the gas finally did reach the matches while they were still burning. Hurry—"

"Wait, Dick—Blondie wasn't in the car, was she?"

"Good heavens, no! It's this way, straight ahead, and then cross to the left."

We went through a red and orange world above, protected by the heavy black shadows of the thickets below. Sand scraped in my sneakers again. Behind us there was suddenly the scream of a fire siren.

It was an empty space, a deserted spot, far from any houses at all, but apparently it did not take long for that red and orange flame to be seen.

We came out by some railroad tracks, overgrown with weeds. "It must be a spur running into the factory," Richard said. We followed it and came out at an enormous block of concrete which had a few night lights within it, a high-wire fence around it and a watchman at a lighted gate. He telephoned for a taxi for us but wouldn't let us in through the gate. The cab came while the fire engines were still shrieking, but now from behind the factory. It was like a wall shielding us. The night watchman didn't ask us any questions. We got into the taxi.

"Quite a fire over there," the driver said. "Looks like a car."

"Yes, it does. Take us to the airport," Richard said. The glass partition was open, but neither of us would have felt much like conversation just then, whether or not anyone was listening. There was first, for me, the matter of catching my breath and making my heart quiet down. Once Richard said, though, that he thought we would be in time for the plane to New York.

So his plan, such as it was, had not changed. He paid the driver when we got to the airport, and told me he had enough money for our tickets, and then, in the lighted entrance, stared at me, looked again and quite literally froze. When he got his voice thawed out, he told me to go to the ladies' room and do the best I could do while he got our tickets, and to hurry.

Glancing down, I was a little startled myself, for I was splashed from neck to knees with wildly assorted reds, blues, yellows and greens on what would otherwise simply have been a rather abbreviated nightgown. The Rayburns had indeed been to Hawaii and Miz Rayburn had brought back a muumuu and I was wearing it.

I all but ran for the ladies' room, my denim sneakers squishing along. I felt strongly that the missionaries who introduced the all-concealing Mother Hubbard in the Islands had made a mistake. Certainly its descendant, the present-day muumuu, is a delightful and very comfortable garment for, say, lounging in a patio. It is not the ideal dress for travel.

I swished into the ladies' room and took a horrified look at myself in the mirror. My face was scratched, my hair was tousled and wild. Miz Rayburn's muumuu was fantastically gay and had slipped down over one shoulder so that my white shirt showed underneath; I was a picture of disreputable deshabillé. I could see my legs, scratched and bleeding, and my blue denim sneakers looked as if I'd been wallowing on some particularly dirty beach.

I couldn't possibly get on a plane like that: I couldn't go anywhere looking like that. I passed a hopeless hand over my hair and a woman by a wash basin saw me in the mirror and stared, and a little girl standing beside her stared too, tugged her mother's dress and said sagely, "Mother, shouldn't the lady wash her face."

The young woman kept scrubbing her hands automatically as if my appearance so astonished her that she couldn't stop; then she glanced at her child approvingly, said, "You're absolutely right," shook the soap off her hands and turned to face me. She took in the full ghastliness of my appearance and said, "You poor child!"

She may have been ten minutes older than I; her voice, her kind face, her whole attitude were entirely maternal. "Come over here. Where have you been? Never mind. I'll fix you up."

She did, quickly, aided by the little girl, who zestfully helped wash sand from the muumuu. The young woman had a large handbag. "Winifred needs so many things while we are traveling," she said by way of explanation and got out a disinfectant for my scratches and a comb. She told me parenthetically that the comb had been washed that morning; she hoped I didn't mind and used it vigorously. She had a compact, and a lipstick for which she apologized again; of course she had been using it, she said, but she'd just wipe off the used portion, which she did, and went on cleaning me up rapidly and efficiently. She hesitated about the shirt, which showed under the muumuu, and then remarked kindly that I must have dressed in a hurry, which indeed I had, and suggested that we remove the shirt. Meanwhile the little girl experimented quietly in a corner with the lipstick. At last the young woman gave me a friendly look and said that if I was going on a plane somewhere, not to worry, because I looked far better than—She stopped there with a gasp as she saw her daughter, smeared with lipstick, picked up the child and began scrubbing her. The child howled—as a formality, I thought—and the public-address system howled too, announcing that some plane was loading at some gate. I didn't hear either the flight number or the gate, but I tried to thank the young woman who had been so unexpected a friend and couldn't find the words, but she gave me a brisk pat on the shoulder and said calmly, "Whatever it's all about—good wishes, my dear." The little girl winked at me. I felt wildly cheered. When it was too late, I wished I had the name of the young woman. I felt as if she were an old friend.

Richard was looking for me. "We missed the direct flight to New York. But it's all right. There's a flight to Atlanta and we can change there. There'll be a wait for another plane to New York but they'll never think that we've gone to Atlanta. You look better," he said kindly. "But what on earth is that—that kimono thing?"

"It's a muumuu," I said with dignity. "It's a—oh, never mind. You look a little unusual yourself. That sport shirt! I wish I had a coat."

He produced a flat package from under his arm. "It's the best I could do. A raincoat. I got it in a drugstore."

I shook out what was indeed a raincoat, but transparent. It was so long that it hit my ankles, but it did soften the effect of brilliant colors, although there was a long gap of bare legs between the short muumuu and my blue denim sneakers.

Richard eyed me, "Not chic, but decent. The gate is this way."

We saw neither Blondie nor Dino, but Richard was cautious and watchful. "I don't think it's at all likely that Dino and Blondie and their little pals have had time to get themselves together and to reason that we went to the airport. But —no, it's all right. There's nobody around looking even remotely like Blondie. Certainly not Dino."

Presently we were soaring up into the night sky again and the stewardess was turning on small night lights so people could sleep. And in what seemed to me about just a short while, although of course it was about an hour, we had landed in Atlanta. In my blurred state of mind the airports were all beginning to fuse into one enormous airport, part of it very modern and part of it with sprawling wings added to the original building and all of it confusing to me and very busy and to the last detail organized.

We found a coffee shop and a table with shining white top and paper napkins, and there we sat. Nobody was near us. Nobody gave either of us a second look. The little waitress

set down coffee and sandwiches which Richard had ordered,
and went back to the counter. Richard sipped his coffee.
"Ouch, it's boiling! How did you recognize Blondie tonight?"

"First it was Chanel Number Five—"

He looked blankly at me. "What?"

"The perfume. It's very popular, very good and—the maid
in Hong Kong, I thought, used it. And there was just the
faintest trace of it in Hobson's curio shop. I thought then that
a tourist must have been in the place just before I arrived.
But if Blondie was there, behind the screen, as we think she
may have been—"

"I see." He looked rather cross. "You might have mentioned these little items to me."

"It was so slight . . . but then tonight, you see, there
were her thumbs. Very thick and stubby. Not in proportion to
her hand. I noticed her thumb when she got out her handkerchief and pretended she had a cold in order to disguise her
voice. I knew then it was Blondie."

He sipped his coffee, thought for a while and said, "Marcia, let's go over that first visit of yours to the curio shop.
Every single little detail that you can remember."

"I've told you everything. There was a Coromandel screen
across the back. Blondie could have been hiding behind that.
The screen must have been worth—heavens, I don't know
how much money. It would depend on the period and its
condition. Most of the things in the shop, though, were trash.
Except for a few nice pieces of what I think was mutton-fat
jade, very attractive. And there was a really beautiful pair of
Mandarin buckles."

"Mandarin—"

"White jade buckles. They were used on their robes. I sup-
pose Mr. Lowry would say the jade was white nephrite.
There may have been some good pieces that I didn't see.
Most of the things were of no special value."

He thought that over, too. Finally he said, "Obviously
either Blondie or Dino or both were in or near the shop.
Blondie probably behind the screen. Dino, possibly, in the
doorway."

"There was that shadow across the door and then the
British merchant said that a beatnik type had been standing
in the doorway of the shop and he looked fishy—"

He was frowning. "Yes. Yes, you told me. Sounds like
Dino. And Hobson said in the letter that someone was listening and he couldn't talk. Whoever was listening heard your

inquiry about the jade Hobson had sent Mr. Lowry. So whoever heard it knew that Hobson had tried to communicate with you."

"And he was murdered."

"It's got to be smuggling. Whatever it is, it's illegal. It means money, that's obvious. And they—Dino, Blondie and the club—are so terrified that murder was committed. Hobson. That man tonight."

"Poor scared rabbit," I said.

"From the club's point of view, Hobson ratted. So Blondie, Dino or—obviously somebody else in the club killed him. It was not the scared rabbit from San Francisco. He was too scared when I spoke to him in the post office. That's why he tried to reach us tonight. The Tampa man, the cobra, could have killed them both."

"Cobra!"

"He looked like a snake—in a raincoat and carrying a gun, true, but a snake and a mean one."

"I can't think what a cobra looks like."

He said crossly, "Go to the zoo sometime. There are still the Chicago man and the New York man. Now, if either of them was in Hong Kong, he could have killed Hobson. Dino arrived in Tampa. Blondie arrived in Tampa. Jones was already there. They must have sent for the scared rabbit and for either the Chicago man or the New York man. There were two voices outside the house tonight, besides Dino's voice. I wish I could have heard them more distinctly. I wish I could have seen them. Blondie," Richard said flatly, "is the boss woman."

SEVENTEEN

"Blondie!"

"Looks like it. She came to the house tonight to find out exactly what had happened to the scared rabbit. They knew or somehow guessed that he was going to come to us. I think that they were not sure whether or not the murderer had succeeded. They were watching, saw the commotion, the police cars, all that. But the man in the taxi might have been still alive; he might have been hauled off to a hospital or to the police station and he might talk. They had to be sure. Blondie must have said, 'Stop guessing; I'll find out.' The other three waited. And believe me, she made them untie her and get her free before they started hunting us down tonight. Blondie —yes, I think she's the boss of the outfit. If she tried to murder anybody, she'd do it very efficiently. But she came to the house because she had to know what happened. So my feeling is that Blondie didn't kill the rabbit. I don't think she'd be afraid to knife anybody, but I feel that she'd be sure she had succeeded. I don't think she killed Hobson, simply because murder is . . . unusual. It seems unlikely that two of the gang would resort to murder. I think it's more likely that one of them is, so to speak, the executioner."

I hugged my transparent raincoat around me because I felt chilly. "Executioner" is a brutal word.

"So," Richard said, "Which one is it? We've eliminated only the scared rabbit really, and only because he was murdered. I think we can eliminate Blondie. The rest of them must feel a little uneasy. Hobson and the rabbit both murdered. Yes, there's a little uneasiness among Dino's pals."

"There's uneasiness among me," I said, not meaning to be flippant, which was a good thing, because Richard frowned and said, "The executioner can't stop now. He's gone out on a limb. The gang can blackmail him or make a good try at it . . . but I wonder, though. Maybe he didn't admit to killing the rabbit. But they must have known something about it. Otherwise they wouldn't have tried to find out just what happened. Dino sent for the rabbit and a third man, the New York or their Chicago man. That's clear."

"Because he wanted help to get the Hobson letter—"

"Or the executioner, perhaps, to help get rid of you and me," Richard said.

I looked around the restaurant, which was shining, clean and normal. The public-address system announced a landing.

"I wish I knew exactly what to do," Richard said dismally. "Well, we only know it's probably smuggling and may be drug smuggling—Dino had all that money. And Blondie, I think, is the leader. She's got brains."

"She's also got sharp fingernails." I looked at the scratches on his face. "She hated the rope."

"Now, don't start seeing Blondie's point of view and feeling sorry for her. It's the law's point of view I'm interested in," he said dismally again. "We—you and I think that we are law-abiding people. The Tampa police would have every right to shove us both in jail. It's called 'obstructing justice.'"

"But we don't *know* who killed the man in the taxi."

"We know they are thugs and one of them is a murderer."

That silenced me. Richard was right, of course; he was reasonable and fair; I had played on his sense of fairness and justice to the extent that he, in a way, denied his own principles. I thought glumly that there could come a time when I strained his love for me too far, and that moment might come when we reached New York. I decided not to think of what I really had to do before Richard made any move of any kind.

Richard got up restlessly and went to inquire about our plane. When he came back he said it had been late leaving Caracas. "They said 'No equipment.' To the airport staff it only means a late plane. To a passenger it sounds rather as if they had carelessly dropped a few seats somewhere. An erroneous impression, I trust." He sat down and ordered more coffee.

The plane kept being delayed; we talked and went over the same ground; we didn't talk and I thought over the one thing I really had to do when we reached New York. I slept a little on a bench in the alcove; the waitress said it was all right, there wouldn't be a rush of passengers until the plane from Mexico City came in. She added, speculatively, that there must be stormy weather somewhere. She was right.

Our plane from Caracas finally came in; we boarded it. Then we ran into Edith again. All our other flights had been smooth as glass. This one was not. I really felt that Edith had some vexatious malice directed at us. In fact, it is not unusual for tropical hurricanes to veer around and go straight up the coast toward Cape Cod and eventually die at sea. She was no longer a hurricane, that's true; she had lost her force but she trailed heavy rain and still a little wind behind her. So even when, late, we arrived in New York, other planes were stacked up and we had to circle endlessly, it seemed to me, before we could land.

The airport was jammed; it was a controlled hurly-burly. Richard finally gave up trying to get a taxi, and instead called the limousine service his company used. A driver would bring a car out to Kennedy Airport and take us into the city, where I was to go to a hotel.

So I braced myself for what I knew would be a struggle and said I wouldn't, I couldn't, not in a muumuu, and besides, I had to see Mr. Lowry before we did anything.

Richard said that if I wouldn't go to a hotel, he'd telephone a friend and ask his wife to take me in and I'd be safe. But if my only intention was to see Mr. Lowry—nothing doing.

I didn't let a single tear run down my cheek; I'm positive about that. I was, however, cold and tired, and perhaps both of us felt a frazzled sort of reaction to the kind of world we had been living in for the past days. But Richard finally put his arm around me tight and told me not to cry, and when I said I wasn't crying, he admitted that maybe Mr. Lowry would be able to give us some information once he heard the whole story, so all right, we'd see him first. "After that, though, I'll put in a call to Filladon. Then I'll see the head of my department. He's a corporation lawyer too, but he's had years of experience."

His lawyer friend and Inspector Filladon would both tell us to go straight to the police, inform the Tampa police, go to some police authority in New York. But first I would tell Mr. Lowry as carefully, as gently as I could. He had to know everything we knew about Dino. That was going to be very hard.

Richard didn't like the plan, though. I thought uneasily of the things I had induced him to do—or rather, not to do—from the moment I begged him not to give Inspector Filladon the Hobson letter. It was all my doing, our trip to the country to see Mr. Lowry. The car and driver arrived, the windshield wipers working furiously.

The driver of a long, luxurious car gave my clothing a disapproving look. I crawled into the back seat and failed to pull the transparent raincoat concealingly about me. Richard told the driver that we were going to Sampler Village.

The driver nodded, once.

"I'll direct you to the house. Then I want you to wait for fifteen minutes or so and drive us back to New York."

At this the driver didn't quite make a face, but almost, and started out through Edith's downpour. I wasn't at all sure that we could tell Mr. Lowry in fifteen minutes what had to be told him.

We settled down to the long weary traffic and the dull sheets of rain. When we finally arrived at the turnpike, it provided faster speed but we still drove along carefully. Once I said, "Dick, if we can manage it all somehow without publicity . . ."

He turned and looked at me and after a moment put his hand on mine; it was warm and solid. He said, "Dear, I'll do the best I can." We were, then, together again and my spirits lifted a little.

The car turned toward Sampler; we slowed down along the village street and passed the two drugstores and the Congregational church, looking very white and clear against the dreary sky. Turning into the country again, we went along the serpentine road whose every curve and bump I knew. We turned in between the old gateposts, once of neat and lovely stone, now broken down a little, with a rusty pipe propping up one corner, and followed the winding driveway, which had needed more bluestone for years. At the main entrance Richard got out in the rain and turned up his coat collar; he reminded the driver that we intended to go back to New York in a few minutes. He helped me out and said, looking serious, "I'll talk to Mr. Lowry myself. I promise you to tell him the whole story as gently as I can." He turned to the driver. "We'll make it short. Mrs. Clurg—I mean the housekeeper—will give you some coffee if you want it."

The driver touched his cap and didn't bother to look at us or the house, which indeed desperately needed fresh paint and was not worth looking at, except once I had loved it and in a way still did.

We went up the steps to the porch with its shabby chairs. The front door was never locked, so I opened it. In the hall I caught a glimpse of myself in the long mirror speckled with age. I then knew that there was something wrong about the house. If you live in a house for a long time and if you are lonely in that house—as I had been in the Lowry house, in spite of Mr. Lowry and Mrs. Clurg and all the chores that filled my days—then that house takes on a personality, a living being of its own. It almost speaks.

The house didn't speak. It didn't whisper, nobody spoke, nobody came out from the dining room or down the stairs. All the same, something was wrong.

Dino came quietly from the library door at the end of the hall and just stood there, looking at us.

Nobody moved, nobody spoke. Then Richard's arm came out; he closed the front door with a heavy jar. Dino said, "How did you get here so soon?"

Richard said, "Where are your friends?"

Dino's eyes went blank. He had not cut his long hair, but he had got himself into conventional clothing, his own of course, which had been stored in a cedar chest. They smelled of mothballs and were too tight for him now; he looked as if he might burst out of them.

Somebody had said something which all at once set up an echo in my mind. It wasn't sensible at all; I wasn't thinking of sensible things, but that echo roused and repeated over and over again: The world is a small place, the world is a small place.

Only the night before, all three of us had been in Tampa. Only the night before, Dino and the men had battered their way into the lovely little white house, set within its white wall and green-leaved patio. Only the night before, Dino and two other men on the Hobson list had trailed us, tracking us into that wilderness of sand and scratchy shrubbery—and here we were in the familiar big Lowry house with the shining banister, the blank space along the wall where once a cabinet had stood, holding Dino's grandfather's collection of snuff bottles, sold only recently. There was a clean smell of potpourri from the big Chinese jar on the hall table.

The world is a small place. Airplanes have made it small.

I felt half stifled. The house itself wasn't right. Dino was there but there was something else. I started for the stairs, thinking of Mr. Lowry, but stopped on the lower step, my hand on the newel post, when Richard said, "How did you get here so soon, Dino?"

Dino's vanity was piqued. "Same way you did but I was smarter. At the Tampa Airport I found that a plane had gone to Atlanta. I suppose that's the one you got. But you must have been held up. There was a flight out to Jacksonville, it met the Miami flight and got in on time. I gather we missed some bad weather. But I knew of course that you wouldn't hang around Tampa, you'd come home. What are you planning to do? Get in touch with influential friends? I don't think so. My offer still holds good. Give me the letter and that list of names and Marcia is free. Easy as that. Come on now, let's have them, because otherwise I'm afraid something rather unpleasant might happen."

A little tingle of fear ran over me. Dino was, all at once, as unpredictable as some animals. An unpredictable animal is dangerous.

In the same moment I heard Mrs. Clurg running heavily through the dining room. She came wobbling, like a ship about to founder, into the hall. "Marcia, they're killing Mr. Lowry! I can't stop them! They want something!"

Richard caught her, his hands on her quivering shoulders. "They?"

"Came in bold as brass early this morning. Came in a taxi. Made me get them breakfast. Then they went to talk to Mr. Lowry. Went straight in his room and talked and yelled and talked. It's something about a letter and some kind of list. They want Mr. Lowry to make you give them up. I could hear him call for me and they wouldn't let me in his room and they wouldn't let me call the doctor."

The man the list named as Herbert Jones came strolling from the library and down the hall toward us. He didn't wear a raincoat, he had no hat over his eyes and no gun in his hand but he was the cobra and looked it.

Blondie came down the stairs. She was wearing my gray, tweedish-looking silk suit, the one Aunt Loe had given me when I married Dino, the one I was wearing in Hong Kong when I came upon murder, and which I had had to leave in the Rayburn's house. Blondie wore no wig; her dark sleek hair was plastered down. Her eyes were serene and blue, and again I thought of an untamable cat.

Behind Herbert Jones another man lounged deliberately from the library and he didn't look like anything in particular. He was nondescript—slender, round, pink cheeks, hazel eyes, a small mustache—and wore a rather flashily tailored suit with white pin stripes. He could be one of only two people, Black of New York or the man from Chicago, the man referred to as Joseph Brown. The two strange men did not seem to have quite the strong-arm, gangster air I might have expected. They did look oddly alike, not in physical characteristics, but they shared an air of secretiveness, of something seedy, something that bespeaks the innate confidence man.

At last we were face to face with all but one remaining member on the list.

Richard moved swiftly; he caught my wrist and pulled me toward the door, and the three men sprang for us. But Blondie went like a streak directly for the door, bolted it with the chain, planted stocky legs in front of it, and said, smiling, "We thought you would come here. Back to New York. Back to safety. Back to where you have friends. Legal advice, is that what you want? You aren't going to get any kind of advice but this: Give us that letter." She nodded coolly at the three men. "The letter wasn't in the Tampa house. The old man says he knows nothing about any letter. It's possible that she—" She paused and looked at me. I thought irrelevantly that Mr. Lowry would explode if he heard himself referred to as the "old man." Blondie went on, "That she had sent it to the old man. I think, though, that he's telling the truth. He asked so many questions. What letter? Why did we want it? No, he knows nothing about it. So this man"—she indicated Richard—"must have it on him. Take him in there and search him." She nodded toward the living room.

Richard grinned a little. "Always observe the proprieties," he said. But the two men moved as if they were on strings which Blondie held in her hands with their strong thumbs. Richard shrugged and went with them into the living room. They found the gun first, Gil Rayburn's gun. The man we couldn't identify, but who must be New York Black or Chicago Brown, handed it out to Dino, who took it rather gingerly. A tiny line came between Blondie's thinly arched eyebrows as the three men returned to the hall, Richard getting back into his jacket.

Herbert Jones had Richard's copy of the list. He gave it to Blondie.

"It's a copy," she said. "It's in handwriting—your handwriting I suppose." She looked at Richard. "I want the real one, too." She took the copy of the list, tore it into small bits, put them in an ashtray and found a match. Mrs. Clurg lifted her head from my shoulder and said, "Don't let the ashes fall on the rug."

A dull glow came into Blondie's eyes. She turned to me. "What have you done with that letter? I intend to have it and Hobson's list." She lifted one hand; red marks of the rope still showed on her wrist. "I'll not forget that rope."

Mrs. Clurg's face was damp and white. She stared at Dino. "God forgive you for an unnatural son. You'd kill him—" Apparently for the first time, she noted the gun, which Dino was turning in his hands. She gave a wheezy little scream. "Dino! That's a gun! Give it to me!"

Dino was usually a little afraid of Mrs. Clurg. He hesitated, his eyes blank, and she charged upon him as if she meant to take the gun. I caught her arm. Dino had changed and was dangerous. She stopped, gave a kind of sob and said heavily, "I didn't bring you up right, Dino. I never laid a finger on you, not even when you lied and lied . . . I never told your father when you stole the brooch that belonged to my mother. I was sorry for you. I—I loved you. So I let you make a fool of me over and over again . . ." She put her hands to her throat. I knew that she remembered Dino as probably he had once been, a charming blue-eyed little boy whom she had loved. I put my arm around her; she leaned against me. It seemed strange, even in that moment, for dear Mrs. Clurg to lean against me for support; Mr. Lowry and I had always leaned on her.

Herbert Jones glanced out the window, sidled toward the door and said, sly as a snake, "There's a rental car out there. I'll have the driver take me to New York." A slight yet frighteningly significant altercation arose among the four of them. Blondie looked at the two men and then at Dino. Dino clawed his beard and said, "Sure."

Blondie said flatly, "We don't need him!"

Jones said, with a flicker of black eyes, "Dino's right. We'll bring him back here."

The pin-striped man said rather nervously, eying Blondie, "We promised to stick together about anything important."

Dino said, "We should all be together. It's safer." He added hurriedly, looking at Blondie, "For you, I mean."

Blondie gave Dino a queerly scornful glance but she decided it. "You mean, to distribute the responsibility among us all. All right. But get back with him as soon as possible. We can't stay here forever." I thought, Richard is right; she's the boss woman. I wondered whether it was Brown of Chicago or Black of New York. Clearly it was one of the two.

Pin stripes said, "I'll go, too," and dove for the coat closet and shucked out a raincoat.

Mrs. Clurg muttered "Good riddance" as the door closed after them. I felt the same way for the moment. There were only Blondie and Dino left, and two people were less threatening than four. But Richard didn't like the departure of the cobra and the pin stripes, I could see that. He said, "We'll see Mr. Lowry now."

Dino started to protest. Blondie stopped him. "Let them go. They can't do any harm. They may do some good. They've got to understand, all of them, that we mean it. I want that letter."

Richard followed me up the stairs. The runner was worn and I automatically avoided the torn place at the top of the steps. The rugs in the hall were old Orientals, worn thin too, but still glowing softly in reds and blues. Mr. Lowry's room was the big one directly over the front entrance. There were great bow windows and white, looped-up curtains, and Mr. Lowry was sitting up in the middle of the huge fourposter and looking extremely well.

He was indeed looking better than he had for some time; there was a cold, determined gleam in his gaze. He eyed Richard and he eyed me and said characteristically, "What in God's name are you wearing? Go and put on some decent clothes this minute."

EIGHTEEN

Richard laughed, a bit wryly but honestly amused. He said to me, "I'll tell him everything. Come back when you're ready."

I was only too thankful to leave while Richard tackled what I had dreaded: the ways and means of telling Mr. Lowry the whole truth. I slid out the door and down to my own room. Dino had been there. He had changed his clothes and flung them all around the room and it smelled of stale smoke. I opened the windows and picked up his ghastly pink waistcoat and flowing black tie and everything I could find that belonged to him, carried them in my fingertips to the hall and dropped them there. It only meant that somebody had to pick them up later, and that somebody would be either me or Mrs. Clurg, but in any event the room was clear of them. Then I took a bath in the old-fashioned tub with its claw legs. I got into clean clothes; it was curious that in that moment I should choose a blue cotton dress which Richard had once said he liked. The day was chilly, so I pulled on a yellow sweater. After I had looked at myself in the mirror and decided that at least I looked normal and like myself, I went slowly along the hall back to Mr. Lowry's room. There was no one in the hall. Apparently Blondie and Dino felt that the more Mr. Lowry heard of the situation, the more likely he was to put pressure on us to give up the letter.

I was hoping that by then Richard had told him everything, and he had. Mr. Lowry's eyes still had that icy-blue look; his face was deeply thoughtful. He glanced at me and said, "Well, you look decent at least. Now then, Marcia, when you were in this curio shop you thought that Dino and Mei were there?"

"May? Oh, you mean Blondie."

"M-e-i," Richard said. "Her name is spelled like that. Not that it matters."

"Mixed blood," Mr. Lowry said rather haughtily. "Well, Marcia, you thought they were both there?"

"I thought a tourist, a woman had been in the shop. There was just a trace of perfume. It's the perfume Blondie—I mean Mei—uses. Somebody was outside the door. I saw his shadow. The man who took me there said he looked fishy and that he was a beatnik type."

"Hm. Yes. I think there's no doubt about it. Hobson said in his letter that someone was listening, didn't he?"

"Yes," Richard said.

"What about this curio shop, Marcia? Anything good in it? Anything of value?"

"Most of the things were trash. There was a pair of Mandarin buckles, white jade—"

"White nephrite," said Mr. Lowry testily. "Unless you mean jadeite."

I didn't flash a look at Richard; I knew that he was grinning a little. I said flatly, "White jade. And a Coromandel screen. A few other things but nothing much, at least nothing that I saw. I didn't search the place."

"Naturally not," Mr. Lowry said, suddenly agreeable. He unexpectedly put his fingers on his own pulse, waited a moment and nodded. "Better than I thought. I was afraid that Dino was involved in something shady again. Knew it when I talked to you both in San Francisco. Rather think I was afraid of it from the moment that piece of jade arrived. But I had to hope for the best and act accordingly." He was taking it much better than I had feared, but then, he was nobody's fool; he had probably felt that Dino was involved in something shady from the time he had disappeared; he had only hoped that he was not. His blue eyes flashed at Richard. "If it's dope smuggling, the only thing we can do is get hold of somebody in New York, some law-enforcement officer . . ."

"The Federal Bureau of Narcotics. Or the Customs office."

"I wish that Hobson letter had been more specific. Well, well, poor little Hobson, he was murdered because he tried to warn you. And me. But the point is that they *think* it was very specific. Where is the letter, Dick?" So Richard had not told him that. He hesitated and Mr. Lowry knew why and quickly put up his hand. "No, no! Shouldn't have asked. Don't tell me. I just hope it's in a safe place.

"These men got here this morning, you know. Quite early. First Dino came in; I was half expecting him, after your telephone call from San Francisco. I knew he was alive and—no, I wasn't very surprised when he came. But—" He glanced at me and finally, honestly, said, "He hadn't changed for the better. I could always hope, you know. Not fair to you, Marcia.

"However, they arrived. I knew Dino had brought people with him; I could hear them. Then this woman came in. I recognized the suit she was wearing, Marcia. So I knew of course that something was very wrong," said Mr. Lowry, sighing. "I didn't know what. They wanted a letter. Dino tried to tell me that he had been kidnapped, he—never mind all that. Those two thugs came in, whoever they are, those two men Dino brought with him. The four of them said that you, Marcia, must have sent me a letter and they had to have it. I said I knew nothing about it. They kept insisting, so I yelled for Mrs. Clurg and pretended that I was having a bad attack. That woman, though, Mei, put her hand on my pulse and told them I was shamming. One of them, a tall nasty fellow, like a snake—"

"Yes," I said.

"—said they had to keep me alive. Just like that. They intend to use me, you know. Threaten you with me until you give up that letter. Threaten to do something that will make you think I'll be so shocked I'll die. Pay no attention to it," he said calmly, and suddenly sober, added, "Haven't much to live for, you know. Dino—"

I snapped at him, "Stop that! You've got along all right without Dino all this time! You always knew what Dino is. Stop talking about dying and—"

There was a faint glint in his eyes. "Being heartbroken? If I had been the kind to let himself be heartbroken by a son, I'd have been dead long ago. Now then, how will you go about getting in touch with the Federal Bureau of Narcotics? Or anybody at all for that matter? They've cut the telephone wires."

"Up to their old tricks. There are other phones. I'll get Tompkins," Richard said.

"I don't think he'll do much good." Tompkins was our village chief of police.

"There's the state police." Richard rose from his seat in the deep window.

Mr. Lowry looked at me. "I suppose you talked Dick out of giving this letter to the fellow in Hong Kong."

"Inspector Filladon? I—I thought we should try to find Dino."

"Yes." Mr. Lowry shut his eyes again. I looked worriedly at the array of medicines on his bedside table, but he sensed my anxiety and opened his eyes and smiled a little. "You've got a mind of your own, my dear. One reason I married you off to Dino. Very wrong of me. I was thinking of myself, Marcia. I thought you'd straighten him out."

Richard said, "All that is past, Mr. Lowry."

"Not exactly," Mr. Lowry said, suddenly irascible. "Very much in the present, I should say. You'll have to get to the police. You're right about reporting everything you can to the Tampa police and also to this Britisher, Filladon."

"There is also the Federal Bureau of Narcotics and the United States Customs," Richard said. "However, when you get down to firm evidence, there's not much of that." He glanced at the door. "The Hobson letter really doesn't say much."

Mr. Lowry glanced at the door too, and lowered his voice to a whisper. "Says enough to show that there's some kind of illegal and dangerous plan going on. Says enough to show that Hobson was murdered because he sent me that jade and I let Marcia go out to Hong Kong to investigate."

Richard said suddenly, "Mr. Lowry, I keep thinking of that piece of jade. Is there any possible significance to the carving on it, for instance?"

Mr. Lowry opened the drawer in the bedside table and took out the piece of jade with his trembly hand. Richard and I drew close to the bed and looked at it again. The carving was exactly as I remembered it: two animals which appeared to be deer, trees or foliage in the background. The milky, pale green was as beautiful as I remembered it. Mr. Lowry said again, "A good piece. A medallion. Excellent white nephrite. One of the hardest of stones. Third down from the hardest stone, which is a diamond. Fine workmanship. Came from the old China. I'd swear to that. But significance—no. None that I can see."

Richard said slowly, "I suppose there's a lot of jade pieces like that—or, for that matter, gold or jewels—floating around."

Mr. Lowry's eyes flashed, dark and intent. "Not since the new order in China. My guess is that some of the people who had jewels, or anything of value which could be hidden, have hidden them. They would be the moneyed people, those who collected jewels. They wouldn't want to give up such things to the new government. The old Chinese were a thrifty race —ah well, all that is in the past, too." He put the jade piece back in the drawer, slowly, as if he loved its cool, smooth touch, and then said to Richard, "It was good of you to tell me before you went to the police. I thank you."

"Thank Marcia," Richard said.

"Marcia!" Mrs. Clurg called from the hall. "Open the door."

Richard was nearest and opened it. Mrs. Clurg had an enormous tray laden with food. I hurriedly cleared off a low table, where she put down the tray. "Past time for lunch. They're eating downstairs. I knew you wouldn't want to eat with them." She went to Mr. Lowry's side. "I'm sorry about Dino, Mr. Lowry. I didn't bring him up right."

Mr. Lowry summoned more strength, more courage than I could have expected from anybody in the world. He said soberly, "It's my fault, Mrs. Clurg, if it's anybody's fault. I spoiled him. No, it wasn't your fault, Mrs. Clurg. We'll have to do the best we can now. I mean, take the most honorable course we can. Don't cry, now. What have you got for lunch?" That too was like him. Mrs. Clurg sniffed and straightened her shoulders and brought him an omelette.

I was thankful that Mr. Lowry had taken Dino's return and everything that concerned it in his stride, but then, Mr. Lowry was always incalculable, never taken quite by surprise. It seemed to me that since Richard and I had taken care of our primary responsibility—talked to Mr. Lowry—we were now, in a sense, free to do whatever we felt was reasonable and fair to do.

The rain had dwindled to a drizzle, drops sliding down the big windows. After we finished eating Mr. Lowry began to yield to the utter weariness which he must have been fighting. So I signaled Richard; he went swiftly out of the room, and in a moment, when Mr. Lowry was really asleep, I followed him. On my way down it occurred to me that the two men who had gone to New York would not be at all likely to have any scruples about any of us. It was about then, though, that the deep uneasiness I had felt since that little altercation between Dino and Mei began to emerge more sharply in my consciousness. They needed the third man. They had said almost openly that the club members had agreed to act together and that the third man's presence would, as Mei said, distribute the responsibility for whatever they might do. It was almost like mob action.

Clearly, too, one of the gang was the murderer. If five of them were in the house it would be not only easier to commit murder again but safer because the blame for it could be better concealed. It would be more difficult for the police to determine who among them were conspirators, and who the murderer was. Yet all of them were certainly accessories before the fact. After the fact, too.

I remembered Richard's very grave look when the two men

left to bring back the third one. So all the remaining members of the club would be present, all of them would be almost equally guilty if they resorted to murder again, no matter which hand actually committed it.

I had stopped halfway down the stairs. Whatever Richard and I did must be done immediately, no matter how, before the three men came. There were any number of ways out of the house. It was only three miles to the village, half a mile to Richard's mother's home. I went quickly on down into the hall. Light was streaming from the library. Dino and Richard were there.

Again, strangely, something seemed to bring back the past: Dino and Richard sitting there in the library, Dino in his father's big armchair with its worn black leather, Richard in another armchair opposite him; they were talking frankly, as they had talked when we were all very young. Dino said, as I entered, ". . . so that's the situation. My father has had several heart attacks. Mrs. Clurg told me all about it. His life hangs by a thread. You can give me the letter, tell me where it is, or that's the end of him. No more than a small shock would be enough to kill him." He saw me and went on, "I imagine my friends may be able to think of some way to make things unpleasant for Marcia. You tied up Mei last night. She's already thought of several rather horrid little tricks."

I sat down on the big hassock beside the table. There was no fire in the fireplace that gloomy, chilly day. The chimney bricks were black with soot; we really should get a chimney sweep before the cool autumn days came on, when Mr. Lowry liked to sit before a chuckling, sparkling fire. I told myself that Mr. Lowry was far tougher than they believed. All the same, there might no longer be such autumn evenings for Mr. Lowry. Or for me, as a matter of cold fact, but this seemed strange and unreal, too. Richard said, "How do you know I didn't destroy the letter? How do you know I didn't throw it away? Or lose it?"

Dino's beard seemed to move, as if he were smiling. "Oh, listen, Dick. You may think me a fool but I'm not. No, no, not by any means. You've always underrated me, you know. You and my father; Marcia, too. I'm too smart for you; that's the truth of it. Listen, would you have tried to find our man in San Francisco if you hadn't kept that letter and that list? Would you have tried to find our man in Tampa if you hadn't know the letter is important?"

"Even if you had the letter and the list, Dino, we could always tell the police all about them."

"But you can't prove it. It would be only your story. Not a letter, and a list written on that damn old typewriter the police have now in his shop. They shuttered it up, you know. There was no way to get the typewriter. Oh, I thought of that. And if," Dino continued with a frankness that was now ominous, "if the Hong Kong police stopped the whole setup, they and the American police—you can see why we have to have that letter, the real letter, and the list that fool Hobson wrote."

"Of course, you knew he wrote a letter. And a list."

"He told . . . somebody. Never mind who. He thought it would protect him, there at the last—" Dino stopped suddenly as if he realized that he was saying too much.

Richard said quickly, "Who killed him?"

"I don't know anything about that," Dino lied easily. "I do know that Hobson was a fool. Scared of course. Knew what was going to happen to him—"

"You mean he knew that he was going to be killed?"

"Scared," Dino said, his eyes shifting, "so he threatened with that letter and the list. Said if he died the police would get them. Said Marcia would see to that. Or my father. And then the police would get the idea." He worried his beard a little and smiled. "I thought it strange that you didn't give th´m to the Hong Kong police right away. Couldn't understand it. But then Mei explained it to us. She's smart. We all understood. Mei says you have a guilt complex, Dick." He grinned openly now. "She's right. It's the only possible explanation. You've been after my wife and you feel guilty, so that Puritan conscience of yours hurts. So you absolutely cannot turn me or anybody associated with me over to the police on a murder charge. It's really funny, when you look at it like that." Dino laughed and caressed his beard. After a moment he sobered. "An honorable man! Hobson thought he was an honorable man, didn't he? He sent that jade thing, whatever it was. to my father. Didn't have the courage then to write to him. Hobson wouldn't go along with us, once he'd thought it over. But he didn't go to the police, either. Too scared to do that. He was right to be scared. But Marcia talked to him. So he wrote the letter. He gave her a list. Now then, where are they?"

"So Hobson told whoever murdered him that it was too late, that he had already written a letter and a list and given them to Marcia. Poor little guy," Richard said softly. "He hoped it would save his life."

Dino's face was in the shadow. I did think he looked a little uneasy but he blustered, "It didn't save his life! Now you and Marcia must give them to us. Then we'll leave and you can forget the whole thing." He paused and said slyly. "And that will keep my father in good health. Besides, who knows what else might happen; Mei didn't like being tied up, didn't like it at all."

Richard leaned back in his chair, in an amazingly leisurely way. "Now let's get this straight. If we could let you have this letter and the list then you and Blondie—I mean Mei—and these other men would go away and forget about us."

Dino leaned back too; his belt pressed tightly into his plump stomach. He thought he had won. "That's right. You can see that it makes sense."

"And if you don't get them, you intend"—still calm and relaxed, Richard uttered the unbelievable words—"you intend to torture Marcia, say, so your father can watch it. You intend to threaten me and Marcia with your father's precarious health. You believe that in order to save his life and to prevent harm and pain and possibly a touch of torture, we'll get hold of this letter and the list and give them to you."

"It would be a very good thing," Dino said and leaned forward. It was only too clear why he was so frank; it had always been clear. They were not going to let me and Richard live. They were not afraid of Mr. Lowry; they were afraid of what Richard and I might tell. We could give them the letter and the list, that was true. But we knew enough to get an investigation started, and that they were afraid of.

It was fantastic, sitting there on that hassock, in a room I knew so well, a room in the house where Dino had lived and grown up; a portrait of his grandfather hung over the mantel. I looked up at it. His name had been Daniel Lowry, too, but I didn't think that anyone had ever called him Dino. He was blond, with curly hair and a neat cravat, and a watch chain went across his waistcoat. He had blue eyes too, like Dino's, but in the painting a little frosty. He looked what he was, a man of decency and rectitude. It seemed remarkable that somewhere, somehow genes could take such a twist, become so strangely distorted in Dino.

Richard sighed; he suddenly had an air of surrender. "All right, Dino. The letter and the list are in my bank. I mailed them with an enclosing letter, giving instructions that it was to be opened in the event of my death—from any cause but especially, say, from an accident."

He said it so quietly, and with such a reluctant yet sincere manner, that it almost convinced me, even though I knew it was a lie.

It didn't convince Dino. He gave a high-pitched laugh. "Oh, no, my boy. We're on to that old dodge. Mei warned me. She said you would say something like that. Oh, no, you can't fool me with that one."

Richard waited a moment; I don't think he had really hoped to convince them. Then he said with an almost solemn note in his voice, much as Mrs. Clurg had spoken to Dino, "I want you to listen to me. I would like you to get out of this—now, while you can. I don't think that you murdered George Hobson or"—Richard paused for a split second—"the man in the taxi."

"Oh"—Dino's eyes narrowed—"so he died. Mei said she would get into Gil's house and make sure." Again he stopped abruptly as if he felt that he was admitting too much, but then he gave a little shrug as if it didn't matter.

Richard continued, "And of course you had to find out for sure that the San Francisco man was dead, so he wouldn't do any talking in the hospital or to the police—yes, that had to be made certain. That's why Blondie—I mean Mei—came to the house. But she also wanted to get into the house. You and two other men were waiting somewhere outside. Then I suppose you expected her to open the door for you and let you in. You don't need to say yes or no.

"Now, in Hong Kong, I take it Mei was in the curio shop and slid behind the screen when Marcia came in. She heard Marcia's inquiry about the piece of jade Hobson had sent to Mr. Lowry. You were on your way into the shop but you saw Marcia. You hung around until you aroused the curiosity of the man who had brought Marcia there. Then you got away fast before Marcia could see you. But the point is that both you and Mei knew that Hobson had tried to communicate with your father, and you knew why. So poor little Hobson had to be murdered. Which one is your executioner, Dino?"

Dino's face darkened. He got up with a violent move, and his big, sleeky fat body loomed before the windows. He held up the gun. "Don't forget I have this!" Then Blondie—Mei—came in.

NINETEEN

My gray suit was a little too tight for her. She sat down daintily but her stocky legs hiked up my skirt, which gave me a tiny twinge of catty satisfaction. This did not last, however.

"You want to get away? I'd advise your leaving before our friends get back from New York. You mentioned an executioner just now. I heard you. Tell us about the letter, and we'll let you go." She gave Dino the slightest flick of a glance but it said, as clearly as any words, Keep quiet; maybe this time they'll believe me and tell us the truth about the letter.

Oh, yes, Mei was the boss woman.

Neither Richard nor I were going to be permitted to live. Mei glanced down at her skirt, gave it a modest little tug and said pleasantly, "Poor old Mr. Lowry. He pretended to have a heart attack today. But your housekeeper told Dino that he really is likely to die at any moment. A little agitation—anything could kill him."

Richard rose.

Mei nodded, very slightly, at Dino, giving him an order. Dino moved to stand between us and the door.

Richard said, "You know, both of you, that you'd only get into very hot water. You can't possibly kill me or Marcia and get away with it."

"Where's the letter?" Mei examined her long fingernails. "Where is the list?"

One of the club was a murderer, the executioner. Mei, though, could be the executioner herself. She had the ruthless will, and she was lithe and strong as an animal. She controlled Dino, that was easy to see; it appeared that she also controlled the other two men we had seen. I wondered about the third, the unknown, the one we had never seen. Perhaps in any criminal group there is one special member, one who can murder, one who will not pull out, one who can be made to act. Rain drizzled slowly down the window. The rug under my feet needed mending; the corner was worn to threads; it had needed mending a long time. I turned it over with my foot and examined it as minutely as if I had never seen it before.

Dino was watching us, but he was also watching Mei for directions.

Richard said, "You're in for bad trouble, Dino, if it's drug smuggling. I hope you're too smart for that."

Dino gave another high-pitched laugh and looked at Mei. Mei didn't laugh. Dino said, "What an idea! Are you trying to stop me, Dick?"

"No," Richard said. "I can't stop you. But you'll be stopped, sooner or later."

Mei said softly, "Would you like to talk to the old man again? He may have some views about the letter by now. He's had time to think over all the things you told him."

Dino said, "But Mei—"

"It will be some time before they get back," she said, with the chilling frankness with which Dino had talked. "But it's getting late. Give your father a chance to decide whether or not he wants them to give us the letter. And of course the list. We know you don't have them here, but you can tell me where they are."

Richard said, "You can change the names on the list. That can't be very important to you, now."

Mei didn't hesitate. "Oh, we've begun to change names and post-office boxes. We began that as soon as we knew what you were trying to do. But it takes time."

"And naturally you don't want the postal authorities to get a hint of what you have been doing and hope to continue," Richard said.

Mei blinked once. She said flatly, "I want the list and the letter. You can get them for us."

"But—but Mei—" Dino said again.

Mei's eyes didn't have a red glow this time; they were nevertheless angry because Dino hesitated. She explained as she would have to a child. "You said yourself, Dino, that your father has great influence with—her." She gave a disdainful nod toward me. "By now your father has realized that there is only one sensible thing for them to do. Let them talk to him." She glanced at us. "But you can't get away, you know. You see, even if you try to leave"—she examined her fingernails again—"you can't take Mr. Lowry with you, and you can't leave him."

"Certainly we can leave him," Richard said. "And we will."

Mei really did have some understanding of men, for she

said quite gently, "Ah, but you won't," and then examined the red marks on her wrist.

Dino said suddenly and rather uneasily, "The rain slows up traffic."

Richard eyed him. All at once we were listening again for the return of the car from the city; yet below all our talk, we had been listening every moment. Richard said, "Thieves can fall out. Perhaps your friends saw their chance to get away and took it. How do you know they'll be back at all?"

Mei only turned her wrist a little farther toward the light. There was another silence, except for the drizzle of rain whispering against the windowpanes. There was no sound at all of a car returning with the three remaining men on the Hobson list. Among the five of them there was an executioner.

Mei rose and walked out of the room. "Let them talk it over again with your father," she said flatly to Dino.

Dino looked startled, but then he turned and followed Mei. He held the gun gingerly, but he held it.

I whispered after a moment, "Is it drugs?"

"I don't know," Richard said. "But they'll not do anything until the men get back from New York."

I said, "They want to distribute the blame—"

"More than that. If the whole gang is involved, then no one of them would dare accuse the murderer because he would then have to incriminate himself as an accessory. They all know the identity of the executioner. And they're all afraid since Hobson was killed and the man from San Francisco was killed. They know that they are accessories after the fact, probably before the fact. Oh, they'll come, all three of them. We've got to get out, somehow, before they get here. But that woman was right. I don't see how we can leave Mr. Lowry."

In Tampa, now sunny and calm and busy, the taxi driver who had brought a murdered man to the gate decided to recant and tell the whole truth instead of frightened lies. In Tampa the police called Gil Rayburn, who gave them Richard's office telephone number and his home address but didn't think to give them Richard's mother's address.

In Hong Kong a young Chinese policeman, detailed by Inspector Filladon, came upon a curious item, claimed it for the police and took it to Inspector Filladon, who presently had it photostated and then returned it to its place.

We knew none of this and it wouldn't have mattered just then if we did.

In the shabby library of the Lowry house, three miles from the village of Sampler, Richard and I made a plan for escape and a plan to get assistance, which, I think, neither of us expected would succeed, and it didn't. It was simple: I was to get out through the big library window, make my way to his mother's house and phone the state police. Richard would not leave me alone in the house with Dino and Mei, and he would not leave Mr. Lowry to their mercy, which was not a very substantial quality. We talked quietly, in whispers, knowing that Mei and Dino were not far away. Richard thought he could take the gun from Dino; he didn't think that it would be easy this time, for there was Mei to reckon with—Mei, who could put strength into Dino's spine and probably his trigger finger.

Richard slid the window open and Mei laughed from the doorway behind us. "I knew you would try that. Go ahead if you like. We have Mr. Lowry."

Dino was standing beside her; his hand was quite steady on the gun. Richard said, "You really can't get away with killing people, Dino."

Dino just stood there, his eyes blank. Mei said, almost idly, "The old man is asleep. You can take time to consider our offer about the letter. But not too much time. The car will return soon."

She walked out of the room again. Dino waited a moment, and then, as if also tied on a string, followed her. Richard said softly, "Mrs. Clurg may be able to help. See how Mr. Lowry is getting along."

He went out of the library and along a little hall into the kitchen. I went upstairs; from the hall I had a glimpse of Mei and Dino sitting composedly in the long, now rather dusky living room. There was something about them both, though, in spite of their outward poise, which suggested that they were listening, listening for the sound of a car.

Mr. Lowry was so profoundly asleep that I went quickly to him, frightened, but it was only the exhausted sleep of an old, sick and nervously exhausted man. It would take so little, so very little, I thought, to push him into another kind of sleep. I tiptoed away and came downstairs. Dino had disappeared. Mei, sitting near the window facing the driveway, saw me go through the hall; I caught a sidelong flicker of her eyes but she said nothing.

I went into the dining room with its high ceiling, shadowy now in the gloom of early evening. The great mahogany table gleamed softly; I had polished it many times. The rug was Chinese, blue and gold and faded. Above the mantel there was a vacant shelf, railed in, where there had once stood a Hawthorne vase. I could almost see its beautiful glaze, its incredible blue, the pure, amazing white of it blossoms. It had been sold to a museum. So had the two Famille Rose vases which had once been in the living room. So had everything of value been sold; only the silver remained, which was too heavy and ornate for modern taste, and dingy oil paintings with obscure signatures. The whole house, though, was dotted with objects of old China, not valuable enough to bring any money, but reminders of Dino's grandfather's days and the days of affluence the house had known.

I could remember the long table set for a formal dinner; the Celadon plates, the sparkling crystal. I could remember some party, Christmas Eve I think it was, when there had been twenty around the table, young people for the most part, Richard among them. Mrs. Blake was there, and Mr. Lowry of course, but everybody else was young and we were going to a dance later and I saw only Dino. He had a moment of glory that night, for Mrs. Clurg and the waitress brought in a huge turkey and put it on the sideboard and Mr. Lowry asked Dino to carve. Dino was in his element, the center of everyone's gaze, sharpening the carving knives, slicing the great turkey swiftly and neatly, asking each of us what we preferred, light meat, dark meat, slicing with deft and skilled hands as if he enjoyed the knowledge of the charming, hospitable picture he made. I couldn't eat for watching him. Richard was sitting directly opposite me; I suppose I scarcely looked at him.

Now I opened the door to the kitchen and startled Mrs. Clurg so that she dropped one of the Celadon china plates on the floor. Dino was lounging against a table, and Richard was there, too.

"Careful, Mrs. Clurg," Dino laughed. "You're getting older, aren't you?"

Mrs. Clurg, her hands shaking, began to pick up the shattered plate, which had been part of a one-time full set.

Dino said to Richard, "Don't forget my father's state of health." Then he lounged out of the pantry.

Mrs. Clurg rose, frightened but desperately angry. "He means they'll kill his father. It may not look like murder but they'll kill him." She went to a trash basket and looked lovingly at the pieces of china. "I never let any of the girls touch these. I wash the good things myself always. Marcia helps me. We never break things." She dropped the fragments with a melodious little clatter into the metal basket and looked at me. "Why can't you give Dino whatever letter it is that they want?"

Richard said gravely, "Because the letter is evidence against Dino and the woman and those men."

"Well, then—"

"They would destroy the letter, yes. But they won't let us go, Mrs. Clurg. We know too much. The letter is the only thing that keeps any of us alive."

Mrs. Clurg sat down on top of the low kitchen stepladder; she thrust her arm across her face in a distraught way. "Then what are we going to do?"

"Do you think—if I try to get to my mother's and a phone, do you think you can cover my absence for—oh, it shouldn't take five minutes to drive . . ."

"It won't go. The old Rolls. It finally gave up last week. Mr. Lowry got a mechanic from Lessor's garage, but he said they couldn't get whatever part it is that it needs."

"What about Dino's old bike? He had one—"

"Years ago," Mrs. Clurg said. "I gave it to the Goodwill place. They said they could fix it up."

"Well, then—it can't take me long to get to Mother's house. I'll leave the back way. Can you see to Marcia? And Mr. Lowry . . ."

"You can't leave us," Mrs. Clurg said. She went to him, her eyes, her hands, her whole sturdy body pleading. "That woman would do anything. And Dino—"

Dino came swinging in through the dining room. "Planning something again, Dick?" he asked with a gay air. "I thought we'd made it clear: that letter or—I can't answer for my father's health."

"You're an evil man," Mrs. Clurg said, her voice solemn yet shaking.

Dino blinked. "Nonsense. Tell me where the letter is. Then we'll let you go—"

The kitchen buzzer stabbed sharply in our ears. I looked up at the huge old annunciator on the wall and of course the needle pointed to number one, which was Mr. Lowry's room. I said quickly, "I'll go."

But Richard went with me. I think we were both suddenly alarmed by the fact that Mr. Lowry was ringing so sharply and Mei was at large.

She was in Mr. Lowry's room but I had to look at her twice before I was sure that it was Mei. Apparently she had tired of my gray suit. Perhaps there was some obscure reason for her change. It was Mei—black smooth hair, round face, serene gaze—but she was wearing a *cheongsam* of clinging yellow silk; it was slit almost to midthigh and flattered a stocky and very visible leg. It was heavy with embroidery, blue and green and orange and black, with gold threads woven into an intricate design. Curiously, though, for the first time Mei did not look Chinese. She looked only like any girl dressed up in fancy clothes; instead of emphasizing her Oriental blood the dress all but denied it.

Mr. Lowry was sitting up in bed. He glared at me and at Richard. "I won't have this woman in my house. Get her out of here!" He turned his furious look to Mei and said loudly and clearly, "Never trust a mongrel."

Well, we didn't trust Mei, mongrel or no. A slow flush came into her cheeks and I realized that Mr. Lowry had been insulting her intentionally; he came of the day and age when it was a mark of low class to be of mixed races. She linked her hands together; she had put on bracelets, too, which covered the red marks left on her wrists by the rope.

I thought, first, in a merely detached way, that apparently Mei had contrived to bring some of her own clothes with her, as well as those of mine which I had left in the house in Tampa. Then I really looked at the bracelets; I couldn't help looking. They were set with green jade cabochons, so beautiful that I knew from my brief education in the Jade Room at Gump's that they must be all but priceless gem jade. The jewels were set in oblongs of gold, so bright that it had to be pure gold; the bracelets must have been made by an old-time jeweler, carefully designed, long before alloys were used in order to harden the soft gold. There were pearls set around each gem.

All of us were staring at the bracelets. Mei, rather smugly now, laughed. "Nice aren't they?"

"Come here," Mr. Lowry roared and reached for his glasses.

There was such authority in his voice that Mei, as if in spite of herself, rose and walked gracefully in her yellow silk across to Mr. Lowry. He took both wrists and peered closely at the bracelets. "Hm . . ." he muttered, peering. He dropped her wrists. "Where did you get these?"

Mei lifted one wrist, then the other and looked for a long time at each bracelet. "You like them?" she said pleasantly.

Mr. Lowry looked explosive. "They're collector's items! Somebody has had them for a long time! That old gold! They were made for some woman many years ago—"

I wondered what woman in history had been so lovely that these bracelets had been made for her.

Richard said unexpectedly, " 'Dear dead women—' "

Not as unexpectedly, Mr. Lowry picked it up. "—'with such hair, too.' Browning was before your time, Dick. Now then, young woman"—he looked piercingly at Mei—"*where did you get these bracelets?*"

Mei smiled. "They came from my dear family."

Mr. Lowry snorted. "If your family is rich enough to have this kind of thing, if you are rich enough to wear a small fortune on your wrists, what are you doing running around with this cutthroat gang?"

He spoke with dreadful and perhaps intentional accuracy. Certainly Mei took his words literally. I had a notion that while she spoke English readily and had an educated accent, she had missed some English idioms. She said, quite smoothly, which made her words worse somehow, "Cutthroat? Yes, throats have been cut. You must all remember that—"

Mrs. Clurg said from the doorway, "You ought to be ashamed of yourself, talking like that!" She brought Mr. Lowry's dinner tray, put it on the table and stared at Mei. "And tell me what you're going around in that heathen clothing for! Here, Mr. Lowry, here's your dinner. Early, but I thought you'd better have it."

Mr. Lowry tucked a napkin under his chin. He said to me in a conversational way, "Didn't you say that there was a Coromandel screen in the curio shop in Hong Kong?"

"Why, yes."

"What period?"

It was no time to talk of periods. I said snappishly, "How on earth would I know?"

"You ought to—ah, well. Now what else of value was in that shop?"

"I told you! A pair of Mandarin buckles. White jade. Nothing else much."

"Hm," said Mr. Lowry. "Buckles were for the tourist trade.

Well, I think we know what it's all about. Don't you agree, Dick?"

Richard, looking at Mei's bracelets, said nothing. Then we heard a car. It was a light, fast car spattering gravel.

We all heard Dino running to the front door. Mr. Lowry had a spoonful of soup poised in midair. Mei stood like a lovely statue in yellow silk and jade.

We all heard the front door open and we all heard Dino say, "Why, Mrs. Blake!"

We heard Richard's mother reply. Her voice was too clear. "Dino! So Marcia did find you in Hong Kong! Is Richard here, too?" Richard was already out of the room, running. But she called, "Richard! There's a letter for you at home."

TWENTY

She didn't know, she couldn't possibly have had any indication that she held our lives in her small hands, brown and gnarly from gardening. I think I told Mrs. Clurg to stay there; I was afraid to leave Mr. Lowry alone with Mei. Then I ran out, slipping on the rugs, knocking my knee against the newel post, and started down the stairs but stopped still to look.

Mrs. Blake was staring down at a dreadful, spreading pool of bright crimson on the rug. For a second it was like the moment when I entered a curio shop in Hong Kong and saw George Hobson, his wizened face surrounded with red. Then Mrs. Blake cried in her clear, frank voice, "Why, Dick! You've broken the jar! I was bringing it to Mr. Lowry. It's my own strawberry jam!"

Richard then had his arms around her, his face down to her face, and I thought he might be trying to tell her something, anything, to warn her, so I began to prattle loudly as I ran down the stairs.

"Oh, Mrs. Blake! Oh, what a pity. Really, Dick—Never mind, I'll clean it up."

I kept saying that or things like it; in any event, I was on my knees on the rug, pushing at the strawberry jam with my hands, which of course only dug it more deeply into the rug. It was very sticky. Richard released his mother, who looked rather startled, as indeed she might. She and Richard were so alike that anybody would have known they were mother and son, although she was small and feminine, with delicate bones; she had a good strong nose and chin and a direct, intent look in her eyes. Her eyebrows were arched in black and her black hair had only a few white threads in it. She wore a raincoat and somehow looked stylish, in spite of blue slacks and scuffed moccasins.

Dino was watching and said suddenly to Mrs. Blake, "What letter, Mrs. Blake?" Dino's tone was such that it seemed only natural for Mrs. Blake to look at him with surprise and disapproval.

147

"Well, really, Dino!" she said coldly. "The letter is for Dick." But then, unexpectedly, a teasing look came into her face and she looked at Richard. "Dick, why don't you tell her to stop writing? She's in Italy now, so that's a good thing. The letter is marked 'Very Private.'" She gave a light little chuckle. "She's probably coming home and wants you to know. These old flames!"

Richard had got the idea, but I was rather afraid that Dino had, too, for he was ominously silent, thinking. His hand was under his coat. He had hidden the gun from Mrs. Blake but I knew he held it with a steady hand. He said abruptly, "What did Dick whisper to you just now?"

I could have told Dino that that was no way to approach Mrs. Blake. She gave him a look which should have scorched off his beard. "Is that any business of yours, Dino?" she said icily. But then a glint of mischief came into her eyes. "Why did you let your hair grow like that? It looks frightful. Where have you been? When did you come home? Everybody said you were—"

"Dead or kidnapped?" Dino could almost always be diverted by a conversation centering on him. "It didn't happen this time. Never mind. I'm not dead."

If we could only contrive it, Mrs. Blake would go for help.

Richard was near Dino, squatting, rolling up the sticky, red-stained rug, suddenly, expertly, he reached for Dino's knees and Dino sprawled over backward. The gun jerked out of his hand but didn't fire.

Mrs. Blake said coolly, "Don't explain. Tell me what to do—" "Get the police. Hurry. Marcia, go with her."
the police. Hurry. Marcia, go with her."

Mrs. Blake was out of the door in a flash.

Mei said, "Don't move! I have a knife!"

She stood just above me, beautiful in her long yellow silk gown and jade bracelets, and she did have a knife, a switch-blade; she flicked it open and said, "I don't really like knives. But there's someone who does like a knife and who can use it and will."

The gun was on the floor, in a pool of strawberry jam. Richard picked it up and Mei laughed lightly. "It's not loaded. Dino never will carry a loaded gun. He's afraid of guns."

Dino scrambled up. "You tricked me! You got me back of my knees. What can anybody do when he's hit behind the knees!" It seemed to me that he was excusing himself to

Mei. Her face did not change; she tossed him the switchblade knife without a word of warning. Dino caught it in a curiously automatic gesture.

Mei said then, "That old woman will bring the police. All right. Come upstairs, both of you. We'll see what influence your father has, Dino. We can't wait. Bring them both. I've— learned a few things in my life."

Richard said quietly behind me but speaking to Mei, "You are educated."

Mei turned to lead the way up the stairs. Her yellow gown with its heavy embroidery swished ahead of me. She said over her shoulder, "Ah, yes. I am educated. I was a waif but I am beautiful. A rich merchant took me in. He taught me English. He made me his pet—"

She had said that a member of her family gave her the bracelets. She had said that she hated ropes and why she hated them. Now she said she was a waif. She had too many stories of her life. I thought that swiftly, and then I heard the sudden scramble and thud behind me and whirled around. Dino was sprawling again down on the stairway. Richard sprawled after him and seized the knife.

Richard had been in the Army; he knew the rules of hand-to-hand combat. Yet even at that moment I was aware of my astonishment that Richard could and had acted so explosively and with such hard-hitting violence when the necessity for it came. Then I saw the gun on the floor. It was a weapon of sorts, even used as a club.

I knew that Mei had seen it too; she gave me a kind of hard push to get me out of the way so she could run back down the stairs. But I knew the stairs; I put my hands on the railing, hoisted myself over it and dropped on the hall floor. I went down on my knees but I was close enough to clutch at the gun.

So we had both weapons. Richard stood up, breathing hard. Dino lay back and looked at him and then at Mei, and shut his eyes quickly. I thought he was faking unconsciousness. Perhaps the red glow in Mei's eyes warned him. Dino had always tried to avoid punishment and he hadn't changed. Richard looked at Mei. "Do you think you can find some ropes, Marcia?" he asked me.

Instantly Mei's face changed; it became waxen and cold. She couldn't have been lying altogether when she said she was afraid of ropes. And Dino was afraid of guns! But one of the clubs had not been afraid to murder. I couldn't for the life of me remember any ropes, anywhere. Possibly there might be one in the garage, which had once been an enormous red barn.

I didn't go to look for it, however, for Mr. Lowry said from the top of the stairs, "Just a minute. I want to talk to that young woman."

He was coming slowly down the stairs. Mrs. Clurg was at his elbow. He could always make the trip down the stairs; it was the going up that was difficult. He wore his red silk dressing gown; his white hair was neatly brushed. Mrs. Clurg caught my eye and shook her head. "He would come down. I couldn't stop him."

"I'll get his wheelchair." It was kept for the sake of convenience immediately inside the door to the living room. I ran to it, dropped the gun in it to free my hands, drew it into the hall and turned it for him, but he did not give it or me so much as a glance. His eyes were fixed on Mei. Then Mrs. Clurg saw Dino and ran down to him.

I wouldn't have believed it if I hadn't seen it, yet I suppose it was natural and human, too. She forgot all her anger, and kneeling down on the floor, she cradled Dino's head in her arms. "Dino, they've killed you! Why did you have anything to do with these dreadful people . . ."

Mei laughed softly.

Mr. Lowry thumped down the remaining steps, glanced at Dino with no expression whatever in his face and said, "Dick, bring that young woman into the library."

He stalked down to the library; he must have seen his wheel chair then, for he gave it a savage thrust which sent the gun sliding across the floor and into the living room.

Mrs. Clurg crooned over Dino. Dino's eyes were very, very tightly shut. Richard cried. "Mr. Lowry, wait! We've got to get out of here!"

"Bring her here!" Mr. Lowry thundered from the library.

Surprisingly, Mei strolled along the hall to the library. I grasped the wheelchair and shoved it after Mr. Lowry. Richard cried, "Those men will be back. They can stop us, Mr. Lowry!"

When we reached the library Mei was already settling down comfortably in a chair. She stroked her yellow silk gown smoothly, she passed a hand over her short black hair, she adjusted the jade bracelets. It struck me again how curiously Western Mei's Chinese dress made her look; it was as if she had got into the wrong dress by mistake.

Richard said desperately, "Mr. Lowry, the first thing we must do is get the state police. We can talk later."

"Your mother will get them. I saw her leave, hell for leather. They'll be here any minute. Now then, miss," he said, turning to Mei. "Those jade bracelets—maybe one of your family did give them to you to sell here, in America? That's right, isn't it? You probably have a very large family circle, blood relatives and friends who are the same as family connections, the way it used to be. Why, in the old China a friend of a friend was a friend too," Mr. Lowry went on as leisurely as if he had all day, and a platoon of police at his side. "Aunts, they were called, or Uncles. Cousins. All this besides the Elder Brother and all his connections. Elder Sister and all her connections. First Uncle, Second Uncle—good heavens, all the way to Ninth Uncle or more! Every possible connection. That long-time custom of family feeling could not have vanished with the new regime in China. And the jewels, hoarded gold, family treasures gathered together and kept for centuries could not have vanished entirely into the maw of the new government. No, no. Many families must have kept many treasures hidden in reserve." He turned in the most composed way in the world to Richard. "It's probably the way it was in the days of the Russian Revolution—the Bolsheviks took what they could find. But nevertheless, many treasures in jewels, in gold, somehow found their way out of Russia, to Paris, to London, to New York—"

Richard had been trying to break in. He shouted. "There's not time for this!"

"These are some of such treasures. This woman can employ many sources. She had many connections. She—and Dino— did quite a job of organizing the little gang, but I suppose one shady contact suggested another, something like that. She has already disposed of some of the jewels entrusted to her. Probably the whole gang has plenty of cash from these sales. I doubt that any of the family connections who trust her will ever see a penny of the money—at the most a small percentage. "Yes," he said with scarcely an instant's pause, "She'll have to pay some of them a little, to keep the supply coming. One will tell the other. Something like that, is it, young lady? But you must have a cache, a hoard somewhere. The police will find that. But you couldn't resist wearing these bracelets. Vanity—"

"Mr. Lowry . . ." Richard tried again to stop him.

Mr. Lowry turned to Richard. "You knew it, Dick. At least

you guessed it. That's why you talked of United States Customs—"

"Mr. Lowry! Those men will get back from New York!"

"You thought of drug smuggling. But you also thought of jewel or gold smuggling. Why?"

Richard was goaded. "Because Hobson sent jade, of course! There should have been some kind of significance in the fact that he sent *jade*. Shouldn't there? Oh, come on, Mr. Lowry . . ."

"Jade, yes. Poor Hobson, tried to tell me it was jewels or gold or—"

I tugged at his sleeve. "Mr. Lowry, please!"

He paid no attention to me. He was in full steam now. "And Hobson was a contact. I knew it when I heard of that Coromandel screen. A collector's item probably. Although—" Mr. Lowry did pause for a second, brooding. "I don't see how they expected to smuggle anything that big into this country. Or any country. Probably intended to sell it to a very rich tourist. Now, jewels and gold—oh, yes. You're an ingenious young lady," he said to Mei. "I've no doubt you would be able, probably have been able, to think of various clever ways to smuggle and distribute the jewels—and receive your payoff by way of fake names and post-office boxes. You seem to have got hold of considerable sums of money already."

Richard shouted again, "Mr. Lowry! Dino and Mei had a private little smuggling ring organized. Sure. But we've got to get out of here and I'm going to take you whether you like it or not. Get the wheelchair, Marcia."

I had left it just outside the library. I ran to whirl it toward Mr. Lowry. Richard said, "These men are probably, all of them, shady jewel dealers, pawnbrokers—God knows what. But listen, Mr. Lowry, it's not as terrible as dope smuggling."

Mr. Lowry's voice was low, sad now, stricken and yet Spartan in his way. "It included murder."

I glanced along the hall as I maneuvered the awkwardly wide chair. I was vaguely aware that Mrs. Clurg had stopped crooning over Dino. I didn't see Dino. I shoved the chair through the doorway.

Mei was still sitting, completely calm, looking down at her bracelets. When he saw the chair, Mr. Lowry suddenly turned natural and irascible again. "Are you proposing to trundle me along the road in that thing! I'll get pneumonia."

Mei had the most infuriating smile on her lips. She continued to look demurely at her bracelets. Jewel smuggling. Well, of course. What else?

And Mr. Lowry was a problem. We couldn't leave him and there really was no place to hide.

"Old Tompkins will be here." Mr. Lowry kicked away the chair violently. "Your mother will bring him and the state police. I refuse to be taken away from this house—"

The hall door was flung open and Mrs. Blake called clearly, "Richard, here's Chief Tompkins. Goodness' sake, Dino, get out of my way! Richard, there's a very large car coming up the driveway. I think there are several men in it."

Tompkins was a good man, a kind man; he dealt with speeders, drunks and minor disturbances of the peace with the utmost efficiency; I don't think he had ever had to deal with a murderer. He turned his back to us, straightened his shoulders and flipped the switch on the porch, then stepped out full into the light, which must have shone down on his star. Richard tried to stop him; Tompkins thrust him back. His figure stood out, clear and unmistakable. Headlights shot up below the porch and stopped. A car door opened.

Richard shouted, "Tompkins, come back!" I could see Tompkins marching ponderously toward the porch steps. Mr. Lowry had got himself into his wheelchair and came whirling down the hall. He roared, "Tompkins! Get back here! Tompkins!" His voice was so commanding that all of us turned for a second to look at him. "Tompkins, you damn fool, come back!"

Mei was not behind him; I knew that. I didn't see Dino or in fact anything just then, for I heard a shot.

At first I thought Tompkins had fired at somebody coming up the steps. Then I saw his burly figure slumped down on the porch and Richard leaning over him, jerking and tugging him back into the house. Mrs. Blake had the presence of mind to hold the door open; Richard got Tompkins inside the hall, on the floor. Mr. Lowry shouted, "Bolt the door quick. There's a chain bolt!"

I bolted it. Mrs. Blake and Richard were kneeling down beside Chief Tompkins. Mrs. Blake looked up gravely. "This man has got to go to the hospital."

"Are the state police coming?" Richard asked her.

"Tompkins left a message for them. But he insisted on coming straight here himself. Dick, he's bleeding too much." She moved him so she could see his back. Richard helped her. Mrs. Blake said, "He must have turned around just as the shot came. Here's where the bullet entered. If it has gone into his lungs—" She looked up at Richard who had got to his feet. "What do those men want?"

"A letter," Richard told her. "The letter that came for me. We can't give it to them. Perhaps we can stop the bleeding."

"No, we can't," Mrs. Blake said. "We can't move Tompkins ourselves. The state police—" she rose. "I'll get back home. I'll go the back way so those men can't see me. It's not far. I'll phone myself. I'll talk to the state police. And I'll get an ambulance."

"All right," Richard said. "Go with her, Marcia."

I put my hand on Mr. Lowry's shoulder. Richard said, "She can't go alone. Help her."

I knew that he was intent on getting his mother and me out of the house. I knew too that he couldn't allow his mother to undertake her errand alone. There was only a vague picture in my consciousness of the hall and the people in it; things had happened too quickly and too tragically for me to stop and look around. But I did realize that Mr. Lowry leaned forward in his wheelchair and told me to go, and to hurry, and that Mrs. Blake was already running through the dining room, for I could hear her moccasins tapping along the floor. Mrs. Clurg was sitting on the stairs with her face in her hands and I had a swift notion that she was crying. Dino had disappeared; Mei had apparently and prudently remained in the library. Richard squatted down beside Chief Tompkins. "Hurry, Marcia. Mrs. Clurg, bring some towels, will you?"

Mrs. Clurg gave a wild sob and began to pull herself up. The men were on the porch now. I could hear their heavy footsteps.

So I ran after Mrs. Blake. She was at the kitchen door when I reached her. In a second we were out in the wet twilight. It was so dark by then that clumps of shrubbery were merely black and dripping blotches. A narrow, thinly graveled road went between rows of privet hedge from the kitchen entrance to join the front driveway. We ran along the grassy edge of it. We could hear the men on the porch. They were pounding at the front door.

We reached the thicker lines of sprawling forsythia, still in full leaf, which marked the front driveway. Here we stopped for a second or two, breathing hard. The foliage was so heavy that we could not clearly see the men on the porch but we could hear their pounding. Mrs. Blake grasped my wrist and nodded toward the long car in which they had arrived. It was pulling out and away, quickly. It was a rental car; I thought it wise of the driver to leave as fast as he could. But as the big luxurious car swerved and spat gravel, purring off into the twilight around the curve of the driveway, I realized what Mrs. Blake was thinking. Another car stood, alone, in the driveway.

"It's Tompkins' car," she whispered. "Maybe he left his keys."

So we crept, like schoolgirls, behind the sprawling ranks of forsythia, which dripped on the back of my neck. The men on the porch were still pounding hard at the front door, shouting through it; they began to kick. The door was teakwood; it wouldn't give in easily. We slid across the curve of the driveway and reached Tompkins' car. I opened the left door softly and reached in. Tompkins had left the key in the ignition, so I whispered, "I'll drive." Mrs. Blake slid in first under the wheel. Then I crawled in and hoped the engine would start without making a fuss.

It did; the chief kept his car in good order. I pushed the lever to "Drive" and the car moved, and only then did I hear a different kind of shout from the porch as they noticed us. One of them came hurtling down the steps. I gave it as much gas as I dared, but he must have reached us, for I felt a kind of thump and went straight on.

Mrs. Blake said coolly, "You hit him but I'm afraid it didn't hurt him. Slow down for the turn—"

I thought I did but we rocketed around the turn into the main road with a squeal, as I did have the sense to brake a little. Then I found the lights and switched them on. It was so foggy that the lights were reflected, but I managed to stay on the road and made the turn beside Mrs. Blake's small garden. The white picket fence loomed ghostlike in the fog. I stopped, and both of us were out of the car and running for the front door. Mrs. Blake thrust it open and ran to the hall table where she had left a light on. She snatched up the telephone and dialed . . . and dialed.

Realization came to both of us. We wouldn't believe it. But Mrs. Blake said faintly, "It must be because my line is on your line. My fault. I'd forgotten. All right, Dick will expect us to be here. You stay. I'll go for the state police and the ambulance. Tompkins will die if I don't."

The door slammed behind her. I flung it open again. I don't know what I intended to do, and whatever it was came to nothing, for she had already started the car and was backing expertly into the main road again. In another second she was gone, the car lights streaming ahead and outlining the car. In another moment I could not even hear the sound of the engine.

I went back inside the house.

My hair was beaded with fog. My cotton dress and yellow sweater were damp and cold. I didn't know what was happening at the Lowry house and I had to know.

It would really be a short walk back there. What would I do then? Go in through the kitchen door? By now one of the men would certainly have thought of that door.

I sat down on a tiny Victorian sofa standing across the far corner of the hall. It was a large hall for so small a house; I think it had once been a living room. There were stairs, narrow and steep but charming, going up one side of the room. A pleasant little fireplace stood beside the door to the dining room. On the mantel a letter was propped against a big blue vase; two Western Union envelopes were propped up beside it.

I went to look at the letter. It was addressed to Richard in his own handwriting; it had the Mark Hopkins return address and San Francisco postmark. I didn't pay much attention to the telegrams.

The letter shouldn't stand up there, exposed and vulnerable, I thought, so I took it down along with the Western Union envelopes, and shoved them into my dress pocket; then I ran up the stairs.

I turned on the lights; in the hall the rose-patterned wallpaper looked clean and crisp. There were three bedrooms: Mrs. Blake's, with its heavy Victorian furniture which had been her grandmother's; Richard's room, kept for his use when he visited her, full of books, tennis rackets, a couple of shotguns; and a tiny guest room, which I chose. I slid the letter and the telegrams into a book on the bedside table, then took a deep breath and tried to keep my heart from thumping. I also took a moment, there at the mirror, to smooth down my hair and straighten my dress and sweater.

The letter was safe. Soon, very soon, the police would arrive at the Lowry house; Mrs. Blake would see to that.

A seemingly strong premise occurred to me: Richard, as well as Mr. Lowry, was safe, because I was safe. The entire club was sure that I knew what was in the letter and that I knew where it was, so they must realize that I could still bring evidence against them. That I could start an investigation. But I was safe here, for nobody knew where I was. Consequently Richard was safe.

I started down the stairs with these reassuring thoughts, feeling my spirits surge. I was more than halfway down the narrow steps before I could see into the hall, and I was almost at the foot of the stairs when I looked across at the Victorian sofa where Mei sat.

Her black hair was a little ruffled. Her blue eyes were bright but complacent. Her yellow silk gown was bedraggled and damp around her legs. She said, "I knew you'd come here. The letter is here. The old woman tried to tell us it was only a letter from some old flame of his. But I knew."

I stood perfectly still. All at once Mei seemed to be dressed correctly, in the proper Victorian background, the small carved sofa.

"Get the letter," she said. "There's no time to search the house. You know where it is."

I still didn't move; I don't think I could move or speak. She looked at me for a moment. The little red glow of anger came into her gaze. "All right," she said. "You called him the executioner. He's here. There's no time to argue." Mei spoke deliberately, with an air of reasoning with me. "Hobson had to be killed, you know that. You know about our man in San Francisco—we knew he was scared; we followed him; he was killed. We can't stop now." She lifted her voice only a little but I knew she was addressing a man in the shadows of the dining room, the man who had killed Hobson and had killed the scared rabbit. "You'll have to make her talk," she said. It was an order.

I heard myself speaking very slowly, in an odd voice, as if I had to hammer out each word. "You—you came through the woods. How did you know that Mrs. Blake's house is here? How did you find your way?" But I knew. I also knew who the executioner was. I knew who had shot Tompkins and why he had been shot in the back.

Dino came out from the dining room. Big, sleek with fat, bearded, his long hair ugly and wet. He looked rather frightened and uneasy but Mei said in a businesslike way, "Give me the gun." She glanced at me. "I loaded it myself. So Dino wouldn't know that it was loaded. He'd have been afraid of it. But he did get up the courage to shoot that fat little police chief when he had to."

Dino's beard moved. I thought he said "Shut up." He came slowly toward me.

I must have liked him once, I must have loved him—I couldn't have married him otherwise—but there was an air of unreality about my marriage to him; it was as if it had never happened. Mei said in her businesslike way, "I told you to give me the gun. Then, first take her arm and double it up behind her back, pull up hard, the way I taught you—"

"I wouldn't," Richard said from the doorway.

Dino stopped as if someone had struck him; his jaw fell a little. Mei shot up from the sofa; her green bracelets gleamed. Richard caught the blue vase from the mantel and threw it at Dino and hurled himself after it. The vase crashed. The gun dropped with a thud. Mei and I both went for it. Mei got there first.

But then she aimed the gun at the two men struggling down on the floor. Somehow Dino twisted around, saw Mei with the gun and began to scream, "She made me! It was Mei. I didn't want to kill anybody. She made me. She's the real murderer—"

He gave a terrific heave, squirmed away from Richard and ran for the door.

In a flash, Mei turned into a fury. She forgot everything but savage destructive anger. She ran after Dino. There was a glimpse of her yellow silk and then the sound of the revolver blasting through the foggy twilight outside. Richard got up and went out slowly.

The shattering sounds of revolver shots stopped. After a moment Richard came back. "Don't look like that, Marcia," he said. "If she had got him it might have been a blessing, everything considered, but I don't think she did. She was in such a frenzy—" He took a long breath. "She was like a wild cat! But the police will be here any moment. They'll get both of them."

It was very, very quiet. There were woods all around the house, all over the countryside; wet, cold woods that night. Oh, yes, the police would pick them up, and then what? Dino would accuse Mei. Mei—there was no telling what she would do.

Richard said, "Now listen, Marcia, it's in the past. Or it's going to be in the past and you're alive and I'm alive and the men Mei brought in for reinforcements are, or soon will be, in the custody of the police. And I think everything is all right at the Lowry place. Mrs. Clurg wheeled Mr. Lowry into the library. Mei was gone. Mrs. Clurg barricaded the door as best she could. I got out the window, as Mei must have done. Marcia, Dino—"

"I know. It was Dino."

"Mrs. Clurg saw Dino get hold of that gun. He slid out onto the porch when my mother and Tompkins came in. He shot Tompkins from the back. He must have gone around the house then and got Mei, and both of them came here for the letter. Dino was the hand but Mei the brains—"

"—and the will."

I told him where the letter was; he went upstairs to get it and I sat numbly on the hard little sofa. I hoped that Mr. Lowry could summon all his Spartan strength when he learned the truth about Dino, yet I was almost certain that he had already guessed.

The police car came as Richard ran down the stairs. He met the state police and talked to them. After a while he came back and I heard their car shoot out of the driveway. "They've got the three club members," he told me. "They're confessing their heads off—hoping for leniency, I suppose. Here's a telegram from Gil Rayburn. He says the taxi driver in Tampa broke down, and in describing the second passenger, he identified Dino. The cabdriver said he was so afraid of the whole thing at first that he even refused positively to identify the murdered man as his passenger. He only wanted out of it all, but then he decided he had better tell the truth and—it's only another link. We'll give the Hobson letter to the police and they'll make copies for the Tampa police and see that they get a full report."

He sat down beside me. He was disheveled and tired, but his eyes were very intent, exactly like his mother's. He said, "Tompkins is in the hospital. They think he'll be all right. I'll make a detailed statement, first."

"What will the police do with them?"

"I don't know how they will work it out. He fired to kill Tompkins. There's the man in Tampa. There's Hobson. The police will decide the procedure. Right now, tonight, I'll do everything necessary for the time being. Then we're going back to Hong Kong."

I suppose I said "Why?"

"This is a cable from Inspector Filladon. We'll have photostats made of the Hobson letter and take the original letter to Inspector Filladon and make a full report of everything. It's the least we can do. And besides—there is something we have to make absolutely certain about in Hong Kong. I mean, see the records and—"

"What records?"

But I believe I knew before he told me. He said, "One of Filladon's men dug up the record of a marriage."

It explained much. "Mei?"

"Dino and Mei were married during that first year when he went to Hong Kong."

"So I—you mean—I never was—?"

"You were never Dino's wife."

Mrs. Blake came back with Tompkins' car and took us back to the Lowry place. I was in an odd kind of daze. Mrs. Clurg packed for me. She also brought me my handbag with the necessary travel papers still in it; it had been in Mei's luggage. Then she hugged me and cried.

Mr. Lowry tried to talk to me and I tried to talk to him, but we couldn't; he finally took a little roll of money from a drawer and put it in my handbag. He really couldn't afford to give me a penny but I wouldn't have refused it for anything in the world. "Buy yourself some pretty things. Wedding dress, maybe," he said, pretending to be very gruff. "Better marry Dick in Hong Kong. That'll tie up everything there and save some nonsense here and—there'll be some things we have to go through, all of us. A trial—all that. It will be hard. I want Dick to have the right to see to you. Now, now, don't say a word. Come and see me sometimes, daughter." He had never actually called me daughter before.

So we went back to Hong Kong, where it had begun. The crowded harbor was the same, the Island was the same, but I was different. Inspector Filladon, rather shyly yet very kindly, noted it. "If you'll forgive me for saying so, Mrs. Lowry—that is, I don't mean Mrs. Lowry but—I mean you are like a bird let out of a cage." Inspector Filladon blushed a little, lifted his glass and said, "Happy days, both of you."